STAR WARS

LAST OF THE JEDI

STAR WARS®

LAST OF THE JEDI

RECKONING
BY JUDE WATSON

SCHOLASTIC INC.

New York   Toronto   London   Auckland   Sydney   Mexico City   New Delhi   Hong Kong   Buenos Aires

Thanks to

Ronnie Ambrose

Leland Chee

David Levithan

Jonathan Rinzler

No part of this publication may be reproduced in whole or in part, stored in a retrieval system, or transmitted in any form or by any means, electronic, mechanical, photocopying, recording, or otherwise, without written permission of the publisher. For information regarding permission, write to Permissions Department, 557 Broadway, New York, NY 10012.

ISBN-13: 978-0-439-68143-8
ISBN-10: 0-439-68143-X

12 11 10 9 8 7 6 5 4 3 2 1   8 9 10 11 12/0

Printed in the U.S.A.   40
First printing, June 2008

GUIDE TO
CHARACTERS

THE LAST OF THE JEDI

Obi-Wan Kenobi: The great Jedi Master; now on exile on Tatooine

Ferus Olin: Former Jedi Padawan and apprentice to Siri Tachi

Solace: Formerly the Jedi Knight Fy-Tor Ana; became a bounty hunter after the Empire was established

Garen Muln: Weakened by long months of hiding after Order 66; resides on the secret asteroid base that Ferus Olin has established

Ry-Gaul: On the run since Order 66; found by Solace

THE ERASED

A loose confederation of those who have been marked for death by the Empire who give up their official identities and disappear; centered on Coruscant

Dexter Jettster: Former owner of Dex's Diner; establishes safe house in Coruscant's Orange District; wounded in an Imperial raid that destroys Thugger's Alley

Oryon: Former head of a prominent Bothan spy network during the Clone Wars; divides his time between Ferus's secret asteroid base and Dex's hideout

Keets Freely: Former award-winning investigative journalist targeted for death by the Empire; now hiding out in Dex's safe house

Curran Caladian: Former Senatorial aide from Svivreni and cousin to deceased Senatorial aide and friend to Obi-Wan Kenobi, Tyro Caladian; marked for death due to his outspoken resistance to the establishment of the Empire; lives in Dex's safe house

GUIDE TO
CHARACTERS

Raina: Renowned pilot from the Acherin struggle against the Empire

Toma: Former general and commander of the resistance force on Acherin

THE ELEVEN

Resistance movement on Bellassa beginning to be known throughout the Empire; first established by eleven men and women; has grown to include hundreds in the city of Ussa and more supporters planet-wide

Roan Lands: One of the original Eleven, friend and partner to Ferus Olin; killed by Darth Vader

Dona Telamark: A supporter of the Eleven; hid Ferus Olin in her mountain retreat after his escape from an Imperial prison

Wil Asani: Part of the original Eleven and now its lead coordinator

Dr. Amie Antin: Loaned her medical services to the group, then joined later; now the second-in-command

GUIDE TO
CHARACTERS

Trever Flume: Ferus Olin's thirteen-year-old companion; a former street kid and black market operator on Bellassa; now an honorary member of the Bellassan Eleven and a resistance fighter

Clive Flax: Corporate spy turned double agent during the Clone Wars; friend to Ferus and Roan; escaped with Ferus from the Imperial prison world of Dontamo

Astri Oddo: Formerly Astri Oddo Divinian; left the politician Bog Divinian after he joined with Sano Sauro and the Separatists; now on the run hiding from Bog; expert slicer specializing in macro-frame computer code systems

Lune Oddo Divinian: Force-adept, eight-year-old son of Astri and Bog Divinian

Malory Lands: Medical technician and scientist; cousin of Roan Lands

Linna Naltree: Scientist who helped Ry-Gaul escape capture after Order 66; forced by the Imperials to work with evil scientist Jenna Zan Arbor; wife of Tobin Gantor

Tobin Gantor: Scientist and husband of Linna Naltree; forced by the Empire to work on a secret project in advanced weaponry

CHAPTER ONE

Ferus Olin stood on the vast plains of the planet Kayuk and spoke the words that had haunted him since he'd left Alderaan.

"Darth Vader is Anakin Skywalker."

It had taken days for Obi-Wan Kenobi to get back to him on the emergency channel. Now Ferus stared at the wavering holo-image, waiting for Obi-Wan to react.

Obi-Wan's expression remained neutral. "What makes you think so?"

Ferus gathered his thoughts for the explanation. *Where to start?* Now that he finally had Obi-Wan, he needed to present the mix of facts, guesswork, and instincts that had led him to this revelation.

In that small second of pause, a new revelation rocked him.

"You *knew*!"

Obi-Wan said nothing.

Ferus wanted to fling the comlink up into the vast yellow sky. Instead he walked in a circle, kicking a stone out of his way in his frustration, a display of extremely unJedi-like behavior.

"Why didn't you tell me?" he asked when he could finally calm himself enough to speak.

"Ferus —"

"Don't you think it might have been helpful for me to know?"

"I don't see why."

"You don't see *why*?"

"Ferus," Obi-Wan continued in the same maddeningly calm voice, "think about it. What difference does it make to know who he was? There's nothing left of Anakin. He died the day he crossed to the dark side of the Force. It was better for you not to have that information. It could have endangered you. It was enough that I knew."

The way Obi-Wan spoke stopped Ferus in his tracks. Obviously the pain of it was still a part of Anakin's former Master. Despite the millions of kilometers between them, the vast expanse of space, Ferus could feel it. He stopped to consider what it would mean, to have an apprentice who would abandon all your teachings and turn to the dark side.

"Why did he do it?" he asked.

"I have my theories," Obi-Wan said gravely. "We can't know for certain. I believe Palpatine has been manipulating him for some time. Slowly. Planting seeds. That's the way the Sith operate. And Anakin himself . . ." Obi-Wan looked away, gazing at the vast sandy expanse of Tatooine. "To have so many gifts, to be the Chosen One . . . to be so afraid of loss . . ." Obi-Wan gazed back at Ferus. "And to have me as a Master. In the end, there were things between us I hadn't even realized were there. I don't have the answer to why he turned. I can only ask myself that question, over and over again."

Ferus blew out a breath. "Is there anything else you're keeping from me?"

"There are things I can't discuss," Obi-Wan said. "Things that maybe I should tell you, after your mission is complete. After you leave the Empire."

"I'm not part of the Empire!"

"You are a double agent," Obi-Wan said sharply. "You have contact with the Sith. With the Emperor. Until you leave his influence, you aren't safe."

"I'm not under his influence!" Ferus barked the words, but it took an effort of will not to touch the place inside his tunic where the Sith Holocron lay. The Emperor had given it to him. So far he hadn't accessed it, but he could feel it in the hidden pocket, growing heavier by the day, burning against his skin at night.

It was hard in a holographic transmission to read nuances of expression. Still, it was clear to Ferus that Obi-Wan was concerned.

"Ferus, it's time to leave," Obi-Wan said. "It is past time. I'm sensing a disturbance in you. Leave the Empire. Come to Tatooine. We should meet again and discuss what is best for you."

I don't need your advice. Look where it got you.

The voice rose from his chest and was stopped by his teeth. Lately this voice had appeared in him, and he knew it was tied to the Sith Holocron. He wasn't sure if it was his worst self or something apart from him.

It was as though he were split in two. He felt a yearning in his heart to heed Obi-Wan's call. To go and sit beside a Jedi Master again and feel the calm of his presence. Yet something wild in him was contemptuous of that choice.

He was suddenly afraid of Obi-Wan. There were too many feelings to analyze.

"I can't," he said. "I'm still tracking the list of possible Force-sensitives . . ."

"You haven't found any. You've investigated the most promising."

"But there are more."

Obi-Wan sighed. "Ferus, the Jedi are dead or hidden."

"I'm trying to help the ones who are alive!"

"You are trying to regain what you have lost." Obi-Wan said the words gently. "And you should know better than to try for the impossible. Come to Tatooine."

4

"I want to fight, not talk. I want to stay so I can take down Vader and Palpatine."

"Do you think Palpatine — Lord Sidious — is buying your double game?"

"It's possible that he suspects —"

"He *knows*. He knows exactly what you are doing. The only reason you are still alive is because he *does* know. He has a plan for you. He is nothing if not patient. He plotted for years. to destroy us. I don't know why he's playing with you, but he is most certainly playing. It is the way of the Sith, to play beings off against each other, to stir up hatreds and rivalries. Believe me, he is working on you."

"He can't corrupt me."

"The fact that you are so confident is part of his plan. He knows you left the Jedi Order. He knows that you want to be a Jedi again. He will speak to you of the Force, tell you how you can use it. He's already spoken of it, hasn't he?"

"No," Ferus said. A spasm of pain hit him. He'd never lied to Obi-Wan before.

"Come see me," Obi-Wan urged. "Leave the Empire. Your mission on Alderaan is complete."

Ferus felt the same confusion again. A longing to listen, a longing to go. But a tide was stronger, whirling him away.

"I can't," he said.

CHAPTER TWO

After arriving on Coruscant, Ferus left his cruiser at the hangar near the Orange District, the one that was used by those who didn't want to go through official check-in procedures. It was a dank, dark hole of a hangar, but everybody there looked the other way when you arrived. Ferus kept his hood over his face as he took the lift tube down as far as it would go, then walked the remaining distance to the Orange District.

You had to know the way to the Orange District in order to get there. If you stumbled on it by accident, chances were you'd turn around and go the other way. The place was full of glow-lamps turned down to the dimmest setting, twisting alleys, crumbling ramps, seedy cafes, and beings from all over the galaxy trying to stay lost.

It was a perfect place for a secret meeting.

They had to scramble to find a place, however. Dexter Jettster's safe house had been raided by the Empire.

Every building in Thugger's Alley had been demolished. Ferus had briefly believed that everyone inside had perished, but Keets had sent word to Oryon that he, Curran, and Dex were safe and in hiding.

That was a relief. But Astri and Clive were still missing. Keets said they'd gone off to check on some bank account on Niro 11, and they hadn't been heard from since. Ferus was worried about his friends. In the short time he'd been acting as a double agent, he'd seen the Empire up close. He'd seen their ruthless efficiency. He'd seen how effective their communications were, how streamlined their structure of power. And it seemed Darth Vader was everywhere. He enforced, threatened, and brought down the might of the Empire on those who would defy it.

Ferus had trouble reconciling the Anakin that he'd known with that terrifying figure. He'd had his problems with Anakin, but they'd been the petty rivalries of two boys. He had seen something dark in him, but he'd never considered it to be the kind of darkness that would swallow all of Anakin's goodness.

He'd been thinking for so long that if he could discover Vader's true identity he would be able to use it to defeat him.

Now he wasn't sure.

Memories of Anakin weren't all bad. They had never been friends, but there had been many times that they'd worked well together. He'd admired Anakin. It was impossible not to. Anakin had been the one that all the Padawans had looked up to. He'd had close friends, Tru Veld and Darra Thel-Tanis. How could he have become Vader? How could he have left so much goodness behind?

Ferus found his way through the alleys of the Orange District. Oryon had set up the meeting using an old contact from the Clone Wars. They could use the back room of his shop, but only if they never came back.

Ferus found the small, cluttered structure on one of the side streets that radiated off from the main ramp. He went in and told the owner he was looking for parts for an old CZ droid. The owner didn't even look up, but jerked his thumb toward the back. Ferus knew that the man would deliberately avoid looking at any of the faces of those who came to the meeting. It was better not to know.

Ferus pushed through a battered durasteel door. Oryon stepped forward to greet him. Trever was behind him, relief on his face. Ferus walked forward and slung an arm around his shoulders.

"I just asked you to do surveillance," he said. "Not the job."

Trever looked crestfallen. Ferus could have kicked himself. He'd meant the remark as a joke. The truth was, he was proud of Trever. He had asked him to determine where Jenna Zan Arbor was living and the extent of her security. Trever had done that and more. He and Ry-Gaul had rescued Linna Naltree, the scientist who had been forced to work with Zan Arbor on her memory drug.

Now he wanted to say not only the right thing, but the perfect thing. Trever had blasted into his life like a lightning storm, unpredictable and intense. He had lost his entire family, and though he had become a street thief and a con, he had also become a hero. He just didn't know it yet.

"You always surprise me," Ferus said, "by doing more than I ask, more than I imagine anyone could do. I depend on you for that."

He could see that his words pleased Trever.

"I wish you could have been there," the boy said. "Ry-Gaul isn't exactly overflowing with conversation."

Ferus grinned. "He's more talkative than he used to be."

Ry-Gaul said from across the room, "Most people talk too much."

Trever shook his head. "Gotta remember about that Jedi hearing."

Ry-Gaul came forward. Ferus noticed that there was affection as well as amusement in his eyes when he glanced at Trever. Ferus hadn't seen that look since Ry-Gaul had an apprentice, Tru Veld.

"I wanted to thank you for rescuing Linna Naltree," Ferus told him. "I always regretted having to leave her with Zan Arbor."

"She's safe now," Ry-Gaul said. "I turned over the

memory agent data to Malory Lands for study. I think we should destroy it after she has a look at it. It would be dangerous if it fell into the wrong hands."

"I agree."

"That day when we rescued Linna . . ." Ry-Gaul hesitated. "This is merely a feeling. But Vader seemed very intent on getting that agent. More than just pressuring her for a weapon the Empire could use. It seemed . . . personal."

That was interesting, Ferus thought. What could Anakin have done that he'd want so desperately to forget? Was it connected to why he became a Sith?

Just then Keets and Curran burst in. Everyone was glad to see them. They had narrowly escaped death or capture by the Empire.

"How is Dex?" Trever said, asking the question that was on all of their minds.

"Recovering," Curran said, passing his small, delicate hands over his furred face. "He was hit by blasterfire, and it took awhile to get him to a safe place to be treated. Malory has come every day, and he's made incredible progress."

"He's already bellowing his lungs out for bantha burgers," Keets reported.

Ferus inclined his head at Keets to draw him away from the hubbub.

"Do you remember a Jedi called Anakin Skywalker?" he asked. Before dropping out and becoming part of the Erased, Keets had been a muckraking political journalist. He knew more secrets about Galactic City than anyone.

"Of course. The great hero of the Clone Wars," Keets said. "He defeated Count Dooku."

"Did you ever hear any . . . well, gossip about him? About his personal life?"

"Well, sure. The Senate was my beat, and it's a very small place despite being gigantic. There was some talk about him and Senator Amidala."

"Padmé Amidala?" Ferus was surprised. But then again, he shouldn't have been. No wonder Obi-Wan had sent him to Naboo.

"I even heard rumors of a secret marriage, but I can't confirm that. I wasn't digging into Senators' personal lives, and I always liked Senator Amidala. She had principles."

"The official word is that the Jedi killed her, but that can't be true."

"I don't believe it either. But I don't know how she died. It was at the end of the war, when things were getting confusing."

"We should talk about the next step for Moonstrike," Oryon said to the group. "We don't have this room for long."

"Before we start the meeting . . ." Keets said. He and Curran exchanged a glance. "We have something to say. We've talked to Dex. The three of us have decided to pull out of Moonstrike. Since we've begun working together on the resistance, things have changed. We all believe that the best thing to do is go underground now and wait for a more organized resistance to rise."

"But don't you want to be a part of that?" Oryon asked.

Keets nodded. "Of course. But right now we'd only endanger you if we stayed. It's clear that the Empire knew exactly what it was hitting in that attack. We've got to lay low to protect what little organization we have."

"We're always available to help," Curran said. "But we're going to be searching for a new place to live in the sub-levels."

The others exchanged glances. Ferus knew they were all thinking the same thing. They'd never expected this. Was it the beginning of an end they couldn't see?

Quietly, Keets and Curran left them.

"Moonstrike can still go on," Oryon said. "We gained three new members while you were on Alderaan, Ferus. And Flame is starting to line up some corporations. She had a meeting with the scientists from Samaria and Rosha. They're eager to meet and exchange their technologies to create that super-droid you talked about on Samaria."

"There's plenty of good stuff going on," Trever said. "It's just hard to feel good when Dex and Keets and Curran aren't part of it."

"We still need a place for the meeting," Oryon went on. "We haven't been able to agree on where."

He didn't say any more than that. But Ferus knew what he wanted.

The success of the first Moonstrike meeting now rested with him. He had a safe place — the secret base on the asteroid. He had almost run through the list of the Force-sensitives. He hadn't had any success in locating any additional Jedi.

He stood. "All right. Contact the others. Tell them we have a safe place to meet. Offer them Jedi escorts. If we split up the group into three teams, Solace, Ry-Gaul, and I can take them to the asteroid. No one but us will know where they are going. Once we set it all up, we'll be on comm silence until we get there."

Oryon nodded. "It's a good plan. All we need are ships."

"Flame can help us with that," Trever said.

"She's waiting for our signal," Oryon said. "Let me see if I can get a holo transmission."

Oryon signaled Flame, and in a few moments she appeared in miniature holo-mode. Ferus quickly told her that he had agreed to let the first Moonstrike meeting take place at his secret base.

"We need ships," Oryon said. "Fast ones."

Flame nodded. "I'll get you ships."

"It's not only the ships," Ferus pointed out. "They'll

13

have to be registered. We have to go through Imperial checkpoints. With three ships picking up that many beings, the odds of dodging Imperial checks aren't good."

Flame thought for a moment. Then she smiled.

"I have an idea," she said.

CHAPTER THREE

Darth Vader left the Imperial hangar and walked the distance to the Republica Towers. He had been gone longer than he'd wanted, and Zan Arbor had ignored his messages. Once he had the memory agent, he'd slap her in an Imperial prison and see how she liked it.

Things on Alderaan hadn't gone well. The Emperor was displeased with his performance. The Empire had looked foolish when the weapons Vader had planted had disappeared. The Emperor had suggested that after Ferus Olin was through with his mission, he'd be assigned to Vader. Impossible! He wouldn't stand for it. He'd find a way around it.

He knew that his Master was testing him. If he could get rid of his memories, he would be stronger. If Padmé didn't still visit him at night in his dreams, he would be able to rest.

He stopped at the lobby. The desk clerk was visibly shaking when he approached.

"May I assist you, Lord Vader?" the clerk asked.

"Is Jenna Zan Arbor in residence?"

"Yes, sir. I mean, Lord. I mean, yes, she hasn't checked out. She accepts deliveries for food. I'll contact her and announce you —"

"Don't. Just unlock security. I am going up."

He strode into the turbolift. He could hear the rasp of his breathing as the lift rose. Soon he would have peace. Zan Arbor was a vain, infuriating, pompous harridan, but she was also brilliant. She would save him. And then he would throw her in prison.

The turbolift opened, and he walked toward her rooms. The desk clerk had released the lock. Vader pushed open the door.

She sat curled up on the couch, facing the floor-to-ceiling windows. Outside, air traffic flashed in the crowded space lanes of Imperial City. She didn't turn. The table in front of her held a crowd of teapots and tea-cups. Tea had spilled and dripped on the floor.

"You have *ignored* my messages."

She still didn't turn. Odd.

He walked closer. He came around so that he could see her face.

Her lips were moving. She didn't turn to look at him. She was talking to herself.

"The formula for the toxin derived from C-tentium is . . . is . . . I knew it once, or I think I did . . . I was born on Moseum, I remember that . . . I don't remember when

16

I came here . . . I have bank accounts, somewhere . . . have to remember where, have to . . ." She thumped her head several times. "The delivery system for toxins into water is . . . I once had a septsilk gown that everyone admired . . ."

She shot toward the table and drank from a teacup. "My favorite tea was tarine." She took another sip. "No, it was hannite. No. Flushberry blossom . . ."

"What are you doing?" Vader roared.

She looked at him for the first time. "Do I know you? I do, don't I?" She raised her hands in a childlike way. "I can't remember things. But if I think very, very hard I might . . . do you remember my septsilk gown? Can you tell me what color it was?"

Horrified, Vader turned away. He hurried to her bedroom. Her dataport was gone, all her files, her records.

He stood in the middle of the room and felt his fury build.

Olin was behind this.

His last chance for peace was gone.

Padmé would be with him always. The memory of her softness, her smiles, her horror as he held her with his mind, choking the air from her, wanting her limp, wanting to show her, wanting to *make her pay for her disloyalty* . . .

Around him, the walls began to crack.

CHAPTER FOUR

They had been trapped for two days now, and the morning of the third day they knew they had to get out or they would die.

Clive and Astri had rationed their food and water but they hadn't had much to start with. They had tried everything they knew to escape the small hidden room in the grand estate on Revery, but they were still trapped. Clive had finally met a lock he could not spring.

He could see that Astri was growing weak. He had tried to give her some of his protein pellets and water, but she'd only become furious at him. She sat, her head against the wall. They were trying to conserve energy now.

"What really bugs me is that we still don't know," she said. Her voice crackled with dryness. "If I'm going to die in a small white cube, I'd really like to know why."

"You're not going to die."

She turned her face to him. "You're not afraid."

"Not yet. I'm just mad. At whoever designed this contraption. Why would they want intruders to starve to death?"

Astri shrugged. "We're in a remote area. If you put in alarms, security would take too long to get here. If this is Eve Yarrow's place, she doesn't want anybody to know it's her place, so she doesn't trust anyone."

"Wait a second," Clive said. "We're assuming that this is a trap. What if it's not?"

"So what is it then?" Astri asked.

"A place for Eve herself to hide," Clive suggested.

"Hide from who?"

"Anyone. If I'm right about her, she's playing a dangerous game. If someone comes looking for her, she ducks in here, waits it out."

"Okay," Astri said. "But how does that help us? We're still trapped."

"It means there's a way to get out."

"We've gone over every inch of this place. The walls are solid. The ceiling is stone . . ." Astri's voice trailed off. Suddenly she slapped her hand on the ground.

"Exactly," Clive said softly. "For some stupid reason, we didn't check the floor."

They both got on their hands and knees and moved over the floor, stone by stone, knocking each one, testing it, rocking it. Nothing seemed amiss.

Astri sat in the middle of the floor, her head in her

hands. "If it were me, I'd want a hint," she said. "There's a lot of stones in this floor . . . wait a second. Remember how we got in here in the first place?"

"You saw that painting and tilted it, and the hologram sent a beam of light to the lock. Presto, we were in jail."

Astri closed her eyes, trying to remember the process. She replayed the scene in her mind. She had tilted the painting, the door had swung open, she'd walked forward. . . .

The beam had entered the small room as she'd walked in. It had been angled down toward the floor. . . .

Astri moved forward. She placed her hand on a rock, smooth and gray like all the others. "This one." *It would be easy to do*, she thought. There would a release somewhere. . . .

She moved her fingers around the rock, along the mortar that held it in place. There was a jagged edge on one side that fit neatly against the mortar. She pressed against the edge. Nothing. She hooked her fingers underneath and found something. A miniature sensor, gray like the rock and embedded in it. She pressed it.

The rock slid upward. It hung in the air, held up by an invisible jet of air.

"Stars and planets, you did it," Clive said.

Astri reached her hand down into the hole the uplifted rock had created. She picked up a small controller that fit in her palm. She held it up to Clive. "This is her way out."

"Be careful — it probably has some kind of a booby trap," Clive said. "If someone else uses it, it could fuse the lock."

She handed it to him. "That's your department."

Clive reached into his utility belt. Sitting cross-legged on the floor, he took out a small tool and beamed it at the controller. "She probably has a special code . . . which I'm going to have to circumvent," he said, working carefully. Astri could see only the top of his dark head.

"Bypass the initial system," he muttered. "Reinstall my own code directly . . . okay, let's try this."

"What if it doesn't work?"

Clive shrugged. "We're still stuck. Or . . ."

"Or?"

"Don't know. Poison gas gets released?"

"You had to mention that?"

Grinning, his face filmed with sweat, Clive turned back and cued in the numbers. They heard a click, and the door swung open.

"You're a genius," Astri said, throwing her arms around him.

"About time you recognized it," he said into her curls.

She drew back, embarrassed. They walked out

together after Clive had replaced the sensor suite and stone. They still didn't want to leave any evidence of their presence.

"Well, the next step is obvious," Clive said. "Refrigerator raid."

"Yes, we need food and water," Astri said. "But after, I —"

She stopped abruptly. They both had heard it. Someone was coming in the back door.

Clive grabbed her arm and pulled her down the hall just as the door was opening. They were racing for the stairs when they heard a voice behind them.

"There's a blaster aimed at you. Stop."

"Seems like a good idea to stop," Clive said to Astri. "Turn around."

They met the eyes of a curious creature — small, fine-boned, with pale green skin and tentacles wrapped around her head like a turban. In the instant it took to size her up, Clive decided it would be a bad idea to try to disarm her.

"Care to tell me what you're doing here?" she asked.

"We're friends of the owner," Clive said. "Eve asked us here. Didn't she tell you?"

"Do I look like I was brought up in Gullible Land?"

Clive shook his head slowly. "Definitely not. I'd peg you for Smart Land, any day of the week." ·

She waved the blaster impatiently. "What are you after?"

Astri decided that they might as well tell a partial truth. She could see by the servant's simple, extensively mended garb and her ancient boots that she must not be paid very well to be a caretaker.

"We think Eve Yarrow might be trying to hurt our friends," Astri said. "So we broke in, looking for information."

"If you let us go, we'll make it worth your while," Clive added. The caretaker hadn't tried to defend Eve Yarrow. That told him everything he needed to know.

The caretaker lowered her blaster. "Well, why didn't you say so? I'm no friend of the Empire."

Relief coursed through Clive. It wasn't often he caught a break like this one.

"I'm just an employee," she said. "As long as you don't track mud on the floor, I don't care. I just came to prepare the house for a visit."

"Is she coming?"

"So she says. And she'll have a visitor." The caretaker looked off to the security monitor. "Looks like he's arrived."

"Do you know who it is?" Astri asked.

"See for yourself." The caretaker waved at the monitor. The cockpit canopy was open and a tall figure in black was striding away from a sleek cruiser.

Darth Vader.

"I think it's safe to say," Clive said, swallowing, "that Eve Yarrow is working with the Empire."

"There's a door off the kitchen that leads to a service alley," the caretaker said. "If you leave now, you can take a back path up the cliff. You can't see it from the house."

Clive and Astri exchanged glances. This was their chance to finally find out what they were looking for.

"We're staying," Astri said.

CHAPTER FIVE

The laserlights flashed through the gloom of a rainy afternoon: GALACTIC LUXURY STARSHIP MANUFACTURERS' CONVENTION.

The convention was renowned among the elite of the galaxy, an annual trade show that gave previews of prototypes and new models of personal crafts. Luxury models could be ordered before they hit showroom floors, and the wealthiest competed to see who could get the fantastically expensive ships first.

Flame met Solace, Trever, and Ry-Gaul by the VIP entrance. Ferus was joining them at the hangar. Now that he was a double agent, it was better for him to keep a low profile. Flame handed out identity tags. "This will get you into all restricted areas," she told them. "We can take off from the hangar here. The salesmen are authorized to push through temporary ship registries on the spot."

"But we'll still need background checks, won't we?" Trever asked.

"They'll forgo the background checks with the right incentives," Flame replied. "The galaxy hasn't changed that much . . . yet. The rich get what they want. Just follow my lead. I've already checked out the displays, and I've picked out our new transports."

They affixed their identity tags to their tunics and walked inside the vast space. Trever swallowed. He didn't know where to start. Every luxury brand was here, and his eyes were dazzled by chromium hulls and rainbow-hued viewports and laser-baked paintwork. Cockpit hulls and bay doors were open wide and invited glimpses of plush upholstery in sumptuous lounges and cockpits with top-of-the-line steering and propulsion controls. Then there were the observation levels with multilevel seating and the next generation of service droids and servant droids and protocol droids. He turned in a circle, overwhelmed.

"Focus, kiddo," Flame said to him with a grin. "We've got a job to do."

Flame led them through the convention. Most of the attendees were dressed in the opulent capes and towering headdresses that were quickly becoming the mark of high style for the wealthy in the galaxy. They threaded their way past the crowds lined up to climb aboard the newest models, to a corner where a smaller distributor had set up. SLEEKER SYSTEMS: THE HIGHEST

RANKING, THE MOST PERSONAL SERVICE, the distributor's banner read.

Flame drew their group closer. "I researched this company. They're new and aren't big, but they have prime technology, and they're trying to crack the market cornered by the big guys. They'll be more willing to make a deal. I've already set up the appointment. I said we were a small company with offices on different planets in the Core. We need some fast luxury ships."

They approached the salesman, a short, impeccably dressed young man in a well-cut dark tunic. His hair was carefully styled in points around his head. Trever saw the eagerness in his eyes as they approached. He was clearly hoping for a big sale.

Flame briefly explained who they were and what they needed. The salesman swept his arm to indicate the prototypes behind him. "You're welcome to climb aboard and take a look. Sit in the pilot seat of these babies. I guarantee I'm going to have to pry you out of there with a servodriver. We've got the highest system specs in the business. Hyperdrives on all models, twin ion engines. But do we scrimp on luxury? No sir. Corellian leather and conform seating, the deepest plush levels in the industry."

Trever didn't need urging. He strode up the ramp and slid into the pilot seat. He checked out the console. Sweet. Major power, full-screen nav devices, and great visibility.

Ry-Gaul climbed down into the engine well. Solace crouched to examine the under-console. "I could install some laser cannons without too much trouble," she muttered. "But it would take too long. The best we can do is rely on what they've got and just fly fast."

Trever looked out the viewport. Flame was talking to the salesman. He was shaking his head. It didn't look good.

"Looks like she could use some help," he said to Solace.

Solace and Ry-Gaul headed down the ramp. Trever trailed after them.

As they came up, the salesman was shaking his head through a wide smile. "Love to help you. Love to accommodate you. I can't. I need the prototypes here to sell. You can see that, right? Can't sell the ships if the public can't see them, am I right? I can get you ships in two weeks. A month, tops."

"But I'm telling you, if we can buy two ships today, I'm authorized to place a very large order," Flame said. "When we get back, if we like them. Fifteen, at the minimum. Maybe twenty. And after all, we have to see how the ships maneuver."

"We have a flight simulator right here," the salesman said.

Ry-Gaul moved forward and waved his hand in the air. "But we look reliable, so go ahead."

"But you look reliable, so go ahead," the salesman said.

"You'll need the ship registries," Solace said. "I'll push them through."

"You'll need the registries. I'd better push them through."

The salesman disappeared inside his temporary office.

"So far, so good," Flame murmured. "We'll be able to take off right out of the hangar here."

"The danger is after we're away," Solace said. "He'll have to explain to his boss why he let the prototypes go. We have to hope they don't rescind those registries."

"Or that the Empire doesn't check them over," Ry-Gaul said.

The salesman came out of the office, his hands full of durasheets. "The credit transfer went through, so you're good to go. These are your hard copies, and the ships have been coded with your registry numbers. I applied for temporary registration, and it was approved. So all you have to do is register on your homeworld when you get there. You're authorized to fly there by a direct route, but not outside the Core. So no joyrides, ha ha. Great doing business with you. Use the manual mode to steer out to the hangar. You're cleared for takeoff."

"Thank you," Flame said, turning on her most charming smile. "You're a great salesman."

"Tell my boss!"

"Will do!"

With a final cheerful wave, Flame headed for the ships.

Solace slid into the pilot seat of one, Ry-Gaul into the other. Trever and Flame climbed aboard as passengers on Solace's ship.

The hangar was adjacent to the cruisers. They powered up the engines and rolled forward. The security check lay ahead.

"There are Imperial guards at the security check," Solace observed.

"It's all right," Flame said. "They're just there for show. They're not going to stop the richest beings in the galaxy."

Trever felt his heart tripping against his chest.

The officers waved them through.

Ry-Gaul shot out into the space lane. Solace followed. They all breathed a little easier as they left the convention center behind.

They flew through the space lanes and dropped down hundreds of levels, zooming toward the hangar near the Orange District. Solace nodded approvingly as the ship maneuvered through traffic. "Good feel on the helm," she said.

At the hangar, they landed the ships and disembarked. Ferus was waiting. He whistled when he saw what they'd brought.

"You sure know how to pick a ride," he said admiringly to Flame.

Now, along with Flame's ultra sleek cruiser, they had three fast ships.

"Leaving the Core with a temporary registry is a minor infraction," Flame said. "But we should try to avoid unnecessary stops."

"Each ship can hold about thirty passengers," Solace said. "We've broken down the resistance leaders who are coming into groups of three. Most of them can get off-world to central locations. We've got sixty leaders, so we've got plenty of room."

They each took a third of the list. Ferus checked his over. He'd only have to stop twice in the Core before heading to the asteroid. It seemed like a piece of juju-cake. But anything could go wrong.

The three Jedi would split up so each would be on one ship. Ry-Gaul volunteered to ride with Flame on her cruiser. They had the most stops to make. Trever would go with Ferus.

"As of now, we're on comm silence," Ferus said. "Any emergency transmissions should go through Toma at the base. May the Force be with us all."

CHAPTER SIX

It was like old times, Trever thought. He and Ferus were zooming around the galaxy together, avoiding the Empire. So far, they hadn't run into any trouble. They stayed in the Core, and their ship registry was passing every Imperial control. Their ship was now full of passengers anxious to arrive at the meeting place.

Things hadn't gone this right in *ages*.

As usual, Ferus read his mind, the Jedi spook.

"Don't get overconfident," Ferus told him in a low tone. "We still have a long way to go."

It was definitely good to see Wil again. Wil managed to smuggle himself out of Bellassa and came to the nearby station of Telepan. He was the last one aboard, clapping Ferus on the shoulder with great affection. Wil and Ferus had been among the original Eleven, the famed resistance group on Bellassa that now numbered in the thousands.

"Amie didn't want to join you?" Ferus asked.

"I left her in charge back in Ussa," Wil said. "I'll miss her, but we have some operations going that need her expertise."

The resistance leaders stayed in the luxurious salon, their heads together as they spoke of strategies and plans. Trever stayed in the cockpit with Ferus. He noted a change in him. Even through danger and chaos, Ferus had kept his sense of humor. But now there was a grimness to his mouth, and often his gaze was faraway. Was it his grief over the loss of his partner, Roan, or was something else going on? Trever couldn't figure it out. For the first time since he'd met Ferus, he was afraid to challenge him.

A dark shadow hung on him like an old coat. Trever wished Ferus would just shrug it off.

"So," Trever tried, "how's the double agent business these days? Are you going to quit soon?"

Ferus gritted his teeth. "That's the plan."

"Well, what are you waiting for?" Trever asked. "You investigated all the Force-sensitives and didn't come up with a Jedi, right? Seems like time to check out."

Something in Ferus shut down. Trever didn't have to be Force-sensitive to feel it.

"It's not that simple," Ferus muttered. "Time to jump to hyperspeed." He keyed in the jump coordinates.

Suddenly a warning systems light on the console started to blink.

Ferus leaned forward. "What's this? The hyperdrive shows a malfunction."

"It's brand-new," Trever said. "Maybe it's just the indicator. I'll do a systems check." A moment later he called out, "It's the transpasitor. I'm getting a failure reading."

"Take over the conn," Ferus said tersely.

He made his way out of the cockpit toward the engines. When he came out, he was covered in grease. "This is the transpasitor," he said, holding the fist-sized part. "I don't get it. Without this we can't risk hyper-speed. We're going to have to land and replace it. At least it's an easy repair. I can do it myself." He strode over to the nav computer and flicked through the star maps. "We're deep in Imperial territory here. Not only that, we're outside of the Core. It couldn't happen at a worse place. We're going to have to land at Hallitron-7."

Suddenly Wil loomed in the doorway of the cockpit. "Hallitron? There are three garrisons there. The space-port is a main takeoff point for Imperial ships! What's going on?"

"We have no choice," Ferus said. "The transpasitor is out. Look, if they don't double check the registry, we'll be all right. You all stay aboard. I'll get the part and fix it. It's a basic repair; it should only take a few hours."

"We're landing?" One of the resistance leaders, Boar Benu, came into the cockpit. His hooded dark eyes were anxious. "We were supposed to head straight to the secret base."

"Engine trouble," Ferus said.

"Engine trouble? Wasn't the ship checked out before we left? This is sloppy! If I ran a resistance movement in this fashion, I'd be in an Imperial jail!"

Ferus couldn't argue with him. He was right. They'd done a systems check on the engine but you couldn't catch everything. The transpasitor had failed mid-flight. "We're going to have to set down. Let's accept it and keep calm."

With an angry look, Boar Benu retreated to the cabin. Wil looked at Ferus. "We're all jumpy," he said. "We don't want anything to go wrong."

"Something always goes wrong," Ferus said. "The trick is fixing it."

Ferus called in the registry, and they were cleared to land and given the berth coordinates. Trever swallowed when he saw the line of Imperial ships. Starships, cruisers, TIE fighters, a capital ship, and stormtroopers everywhere.

"This is one crazy new moon day," he whispered. "Bad luck would be *good* luck compared to this."

"It's okay," Ferus said steadily. "We can do this. I'll just wheel us into the hangar, and we'll keep a low profile."

He slid the cruiser into a slot. The resistance leaders looked up as he poked his head in the cabin.

"We've taken a vote," Boar Benu said. "If you don't

return and the ship isn't fixed in one hour, we're all splitting up and finding transport back to our own worlds."

How dare you defy me?

There was that voice again. Ferus kept his breathing even.

"That's more dangerous than waiting," he protested.

"We've had to scramble before," Boar said. "That doesn't worry us. Sitting here and waiting to be arrested is worse."

"I'll get you off the planet in an hour," Ferus said.

"We should act as normally as possible," Boar said. "My suggestion is that we head for the cantina, as though this were a routine stop for repairs."

"I think you should stay aboard," Ferus said. "You'll attract less attention that way."

"If they check that registry and find out it's temporary we'll be in trouble," Boar said. "We'd rather be in a position to jump on a passenger ship if we have to."

Ferus inclined his head. He couldn't tell them what to do, unfortunately.

Wil caught up to him as he was leaving the craft. "I tried to reason with them. Boar has spooked them. He doesn't trust you."

Trever said, "He's pretty jittery for a resistance leader."

"I don't blame him," Ferus said. "There's a lot to be jittery about. But we've gone through too much to have everything fall apart now. If I'm not back in an hour, steal a ship and take off."

Ferus strode through the hangar, heading for the bank of turbolifts that led to the surface of the planet. He counted on there being plenty of repair shops close to the busy spaceport. That was a given. But he also had to find a place where questions weren't asked. Luckily, places that sold parts were usually that way.

As the turbolift dropped, Ferus felt the motion as though he were free-falling. He once again had the sense that his mind was dividing. It was happening more frequently now. Several times on the trip he had to restrain himself from telling Trever brusquely to stop asking questions. He remembered a time not long ago when he'd enjoyed Trever's talk. He had known it sprang from a combination of youth and nervousness and affection, and had joined in with the boy's banter. Now it just made his brain explode.

When Boar had told him that they had taken a vote to leave if he didn't succeed, he had felt fury out of proportion to the decision. The anger had been startling.

The turbolift doors opened. Ferus felt the breeze on his damp neck. The feelings were caused by the Sith Holocron, he knew. The trick was not to be intimidated by them. If he was going to learn how to draw power from the dark side of the Force, then he was going to have to navigate some bumpy waters.

When Wil had touched his arm as he was leaving, Ferus has also experienced a flare of anger. For a moment, Wil had seemed like a shadow, and Ferus had looked at Wil and Trever as though they were behind a screen. He had felt no emotion for them except anger.

It wasn't him. It wasn't him at all.

Of course it is you.

Recognize it and begin the journey to what you can be.

You are learning that others just impede your progress.

CHAPTER SEVEN

Clive and Astri were well-hidden, but when Darth Vader entered, Clive wondered if they really were as secure as he thought. They had ducked into the bedroom. If Vader came upstairs, they would be able to slip out the window and jump down to the soft ground below.

They could hear him questioning the servant, his voice terse and his usual deep monotone full of annoyance.

"She was supposed to meet me here. Are you telling me she's not coming?"

"I don't know, Lord Vader. She contacted me yesterday and told me to ready the house. She didn't say when she'd arrive. She doesn't give me her schedule."

A long silence stretched out for a moment that must have terrified the servant.

"Go about your duties, then," Vader said.

Clive put his eye to the crack in the door. The servant scurried off to the other wing of the house. Vader activated his comlink.

"Yarrow is *not* here," he said. "No message here for me, either."

Clive couldn't see the holo-image, but he recognized Emperor Palpatine's voice. "Are you telling me that Twilight must be cancelled?"

"It is already in play. It is time to awaken our mole. Then I will check the emergency drop."

"Nothing had better go wrong this time," the Emperor said.

"I am proceeding . . ." Vader's footsteps sounded, the clack of his boots on stones, and Clive kept missing words. ". . . Bespin system . . . Coruscant." The footsteps paused. "The preliminary weapon will be tested and Twilight will come to a close."

Clive couldn't hear the Emperor's response. He heard the sound of Vader's boots again. With relief, he recognized the sound of the front door opening. Astri let out the breath she'd been holding.

The door didn't close.

Vader was standing there. Waiting.

The servant's footsteps came down the hall. "Is there anything else I can do for you, sir?"

"Has anyone come to visit here besides me?"

"No visitors here. I mean, aside from herself. She got this place for peace and quiet, she told me, so there's never any visitors here. Oh, except for yourself, Lord Vader. And me, I suppose, though I'm not a visitor, technically —"

Vader must have grown impatient of the servant's bumbling manner. Clive heard his footsteps on the gravel.

Moments later an agitated caretaker opened the bedroom door. "He's taken off. You'd better be going. Do me a favor." She thrust a bag of food into their hands. "Don't come back."

"Don't worry," Clive said. "We won't."

The way back to their craft was slower than the way down. They hiked up the steep, overgrown trail, occasionally having to scale sheer rocky cliffs.

"I couldn't tell what all that was about," Astri said. "But I know we got some crucial nuggets of information."

"Twilight again," Clive said. "We've got to contact Ferus. We've got pieces of the puzzle, maybe he can put it together."

As soon as they got to the ship, they tried to contact Ferus. No luck. Solace, Ry-Gaul, Dexter's safe house . . . no answer anywhere.

"Strange," Clive said. "I don't like this."

"We're going to have to try Toma at the base," Astri said. "I know we're only supposed to do that in an emergency, but this qualifies."

Luckily they were able to get through. Toma's voice was faint but distinct.

"They're all on comm silence," he said. "They picked up some new ships at the Galactic Luxury Cruiser

Convention, and they're all heading here. And the safe house is gone. Dex, Curran, and Keets are in hiding. That's all I know."

Something pinged inside Clive's head, an *a-ha!* memory. It flashed fully formed into his brain. At last he remembered what he'd been struggling to recall.

"The Galactic Luxury Cruiser Convention!" he said. "That's where I saw her!"

"Eve?" Astri asked.

"Flame! She is Eve Yarrow! I always knew she looked familiar. And that time she was wounded on Bellassa and I saw her lying down, with her eyes closed — she looked really familiar. I was there at the convention — maybe five years ago — and Eve Yarrow got hit accidentally by a prototype airspeeder that went hairy. She was knocked out for a minute — it caused all kinds of commotion. I helped her up. I remember her now — the hair is different — but it's Flame!"

"And Vader was just here for a meeting with Eve Yarrow." Astri looked stricken. "Flame is an Imperial agent!"

Toma's voice crackled from the comm. "Are you still there?"

Clive leaned in and spoke urgently. "You must tell Ferus to contact us," Clive said. "He must delay the meeting. Flame is an enemy agent. Don't bring anyone to the base." They were losing the connection now. "Do you read me? Flame is an agent of the Empire!"

To his relief, Toma's voice came through. "I read you. Flame is the enemy. The storm's intensifying — I'm going to lose the signal, but I'll keep trying. Don't worry."

As the communication ended, Clive turned to Astri. "The guy must be kidding. Worrying is all I do."

Vader set the coordinates and settled in for the trip back to Coruscant. He would let his fury leave him now, but he would recall it when he saw Eve again. This operation was in jeopardy, and it could not fail.

The comm unit blinked, and he saw it was from a high-ranking member of the Security Corps. He had enlisted him to monitor reports over the security channel for certain areas he was keeping an eye on.

"Lord Vader, something has come up in the Niro 11 segment."

"What is it?"

"Just a routine police matter, sir, but —"

"Do not interpret it for me," Vader spit out. "Just tell me what it is."

"The theft of a space cruiser. A human man and woman entered the bank posing as a wealthy couple. We believe their purpose was to rob an account until security showed up to do a routine check. They left and stole the cruiser of a bank employee named . . . Herk Bloomi."

"They escaped?"

"It wasn't clear at the time that they were criminals."

"Do we know what account they were attempting to infiltrate?"

"I don't have that information, sir. According to Bloomi, they hadn't gotten far enough in their scam."

"I want Bloomi under interrogation *now*. Make sure he is telling the truth. Do you have the cruiser's registry numbers?"

"Of course. It's been reported as stolen."

"Put it through the highest security search. I want that ship." Vader closed the communication. It could mean nothing — but he didn't like the coincidence. Eve Yarrow's accounts were on Niro 11. And just now, he'd felt something was amiss at her retreat.

Someone was on Eve Yarrow's tail.

He activated the comm unit again. In a moment, Hydra's hologram shimmered. "I am at your service, Lord Vader."

"Where is Olin?"

"We completed our investigations, and he went back to Coruscant to receive our next orders."

"Have you heard from him since he returned?"

"No, Lord Vader. I am scheduled to meet with him after I tie up some loose ends here."

"Forget your orders. I need you to track this ship." Vader recited the registry numbers. "Detain the ship and arrest whoever is aboard. Give this your highest priority."

"Yes, Lord Vader."

"This is your last chance to redeem yourself. Things on Alderaan did not go well. Contact me when it is done. Then I might have need of you again."

Vader blasted into hyperspace. He had to return to Coruscant.

CHAPTER EIGHT

Ferus bypassed the parts stores that advertised their gleaming wares in organized rows on ramps that brought your order seconds after you keyed it in. He was looking for an older shop, a little cluttered, that wasn't doing so well and would be glad for the business. He found it about a half a kilometer from the spaceport, in a run-down area that had seen better days. He passed a droid repair shop, a messenger service, and a takeout tea shop. Then he saw it — a grimy laser sign blinking TUTEN'S STARS IP REPA RS. He figured if a repair shop couldn't be bothered to repair its own sign, it would be a safe bet that the people inside would help him without asking too many questions.

He entered the shop. A humanoid male came out from behind a battered desk heaped with oily parts. His thick-fingered hands were black with grease. Even his cranial crown was black and oily, looking more like a spare part of a ship than a part of his body. Ferus recognized him as a Koorivar. He had heard that there were plans to shift many non-human species out of the Core Worlds and move them farther out among the Mid-Rim worlds. He imagined that this proprietor wouldn't be a fan of the Emperor.

"Tuten at your service," the Koorivar said. "We have everything you need, everything guaranteed."

Ferus looked around the cluttered shop. He wondered how Tuten could find anything here. "I need a transpasitor."

"Not a problem, I have many over here. I always keep many models in stock. Let me show you and you can choose." Tuten led Ferus over to a wallful of drawers, some huge, some tiny. Spilling out of them were various tools and parts. Ferus kicked through a pile of greasy rags to get to the drawer. He was beginning to regret his decision to come here. What if the parts were defective?

As if Tuten had caught his thought, he pulled open the door with a flourish. "What the others don't understand is, grease makes these parts work. You slip them right into your engine, power up, and they hum like babies. Look, I only procure the best for my customers."

Ferus scanned the parts. He wasn't an expert, but he knew engines. These parts looked in good shape. He ran his fingers along the transpasitor, searching for the telltale seam that would mean it had been re-welded.

"No re-welded parts in this drawer. Only the best. Did you come through a magnetic storm on the way here? Because that can make them go wonky if they're not calibrated just so by a good mechanic, not a smidge off because if not . . . poof, bam, smoke, and you're in trouble. These new models with the twin ion engines, very fancy, right? But they don't tell you about that, do they?"

"I'll take this one."

"Excellent choice. Discerning customer. I like that." Tuten smiled, and Ferus wished he hadn't. His teeth were as black as his cranial crown.

Ferus followed him back to his cluttered desk. Tuten reached under and fished out a battered datapad from the pile. "Okay, just the routine questions. ID registry number of ship?"

Ferus knew this was coming. The Empire was trying out a new policy at major spaceports, forcing parts dealers to obtain ship registry numbers for major parts requests. It was just another way to keep up with ships going in and out, just another regulation, just another tax.

And just another way for the Empire to track his ship.

He leaned over the counter, holding credits in his hand. "Do we really need to do this? It's such a small part. It would fit in my pocket, and I could walk out of here."

"True, true. And regulations are so . . . pushy. What a bunch of meddlers, those officials are."

"All that paperwork for just a transpasitor."

Tuten eyed the credits. "Transpasitors are expensive . . ."

"Getting more expensive all the time." Ferus added more credits to the pile.

Tuten grabbed them. "Now, since we've made such a nice deal, I'll tell you what I'll do. I'll throw in a re-welded one as a backup. Then you tell everyone you know to come to Tuten's, to get the best deal in the Mid-Rim. Hang on."

Tuten disappeared into the back storeroom. Ferus put the transpasitor in his pocket. He waited a moment, and then another.

And then he got a very uneasy feeling.

Maybe it was time to go.

He looked out the dusty front window. Two stormtroopers were pulling up in a landspeeder.

Ferus vaulted over the counter and ran into the back. Tuten had wedged himself between two towering piles of junk and was trying to look invisible. His eyes widened when he saw Ferus. "Sorry!" he whispered. "They threatened to close my shop if I don't inform! Anybody who doesn't want me to give the registry numbers, I have to tell. Sorry!"

Ferus ignored him and headed for the back exit. He entered the back alley just as one of the stormtroopers rounded the corner, blaster in hand. Ferus leaped, avoiding the blaster fire that struck the door, leaving it a smoking wreck. He ran along the top of the wall and then leaped onto the next roof, blasterfire streaking the air behind him. He could feel the heat at his back.

This wasn't good. He meant to just slip in and out, fix the ship, and be off. Now he had stormtroopers on his tail, and he couldn't lead them back to the spaceport.

Ferus leaped down from the roof into the next alley. He saw that a maze of alleys ran behind all the shops, connecting them to a utility lane on one side.

One of the skills he'd learned as a Jedi was a practical one — Jedi didn't get lost. He'd had enough memory drills at the Temple, exercises called "urban pursuit" in which he'd had to memorize a map of a large city in a matter of minutes and then plot an escape route in a matter of seconds, following a trial run through the streets of a quadrant of Galactic City.

So a twisting maze of alleys shouldn't have been a problem.

He had an advantage. He was on foot, and the stormtroopers were in a landspeeder. What they gained in speed they lost in maneuverability on the narrow passageways, some barely wider than his shoulders. He ran, dodging garbage and the occasional surprised proprietor leaning against his or her back stoop. In his mind he kept the location of the spaceport firmly fixed, even as he turned left, right, then left again in a series of twists and switchbacks. Sometimes he could hear the hum of the landspeeder's repulsorlift engine but he would double back and dodge behind a convenient heap of parts or garbage and the noise would grow fainter.

Things would have been fine — well, not fine, but doable — if he hadn't run out of alleyways. And if he hadn't heard the doubling, then tripling, of engine noise. Airspeeders now, capable of flying over the alleyways. They'd sent in reinforcements.

Ferus knew now that he'd eventually be cornered. He couldn't outrun this amount of Imperial support.

He could hear the noise of the engines as they circled, waiting for him to emerge. He would be spotted as soon as he did. The landspeeder was in the next alley, searching for him, hoping to drive him out.

He contacted Trever on his comlink. The boy sounded relieved when he heard his voice.

"Did you get the transpasitor?" Trever asked.

"Got it."

"Good. Is everything okay?"

"Great," Ferus said, wincing as another airspeeder buzzed overhead. "Where are our passengers?"

"They went to the cantina. Wil and I are on the ship, but we're about to follow."

Ferus thought quickly. "All right. Find tables on the terrace, the one nearest to the runway. And watch for me. When I give the signal, get everyone aboard."

"Okay, got it," Trever said. "We'll be ready."

Ferus doubled back down the end of the alley. He recognized that he'd come full circle. He was looking for something now, a business he'd seen on the way to the repair shop. He scanned the signs over the doorways, trying to decipher the faded and missing letters. He stopped in front of SPEEDZING MESSENG RZ 4 ALL YO R NEEDZ.

A pen held a battered array of swoops. A group of youths loitered around them, leaning against the walls of the building. They watched Ferus with flat gazes. He knew that often messenger boys and girls were recruited from the poorer sections of cities, paid little and worked hard, with long hours and much abuse. On some planets with aging communications systems and frequent planetary atmospheric disturbances, it was sometimes faster and easier to employ a messenger than rely on the comm network.

Ferus nodded at several members of the group. He picked out the one with the most obvious attitude, the one who looked him up and down with a hostile expression.

"Who's the fastest here?" he asked.

"Ditto," one of the kids said, jerking his chin toward the boy Ferus was eyeing. "He's the one."

Ferus gave a quick look at the battered swoops. They were basically engines with seats and handlebars. "On these machines?"

"If you got the stuff, it shouldn't matter what you're sitting on," the boy named Ditto said. "But not many have the stuff."

"So, do you think you do?" Ferus asked him.

"Said I did, didn't I?"

"Because I've got a job that pays, but I need some-one who's not only fast, but who can maneuver through traffic. Heavy traffic."

Ditto rolled his eyes. "Space traffic is easy. If you go fast enough, the others just get out of your way."

"Even stormtroopers?"

"Stormtroopers?" the boy snorted. "They only think they know how to drive."

The girl standing next to Ditto spoke up. She had short, spiky red hair and a dust-streaked face. "You've got to clear all jobs through the boss." She jerked her chin. "Inside."

"I don't want to go through your boss."

The group fell silent. Ferus knew what he was ask-ing. If anyone did a job for him, they'd risk dismissal. "But the job will take less than three minutes. Ditto here would be the first rider, but I need the rest of you, too. I'll pay triple rates."

"This is becoming an almost interesting proposi-tion," Ditto said.

The girl looked him up and down. "We better see the credits first."

Ferus reached into his pocket. Luckily Flame had given them all substantial amounts of credits before they'd left.

"Who wants to work for me?" he asked.

All the boys and girls crowded close. Ferus handed out credits. "You'll get the second half at the spaceport, at the terrace at the cantina."

The rest of the messengers looked at Ditto and the girl. They seemed to be the leaders. Ferus waited, watching them. Ditto and the girl stared at him, trying to make a judgment as they held the credits in their fists.

"Why not?" Ditto said. "It's been a slow day."

The crowd of swoops rose into the air like birds, with Ditto in the lead. Ferus stayed in the middle of the flock, flying so close to the others that he could have reached out and touched his neighbor's elbow. He'd borrowed an old cap, pulled it down on his head the way the others did, and kept his head low, the wind in his face.

The red-haired girl, Laurn, who turned out to be Ditto's sister, flew next to him. They flew fast, straight up out of the alley district. The airspeeders full of stormtroopers came close to check them out, but the messengers only laughed. They buzzed close to the airspeeders, circled around, dived, and climbed, zooming away as the stormtroopers ignored them and still kept a tight cordon on the area. They were used to the antics of the messenger fleet.

The fleet kept close ranks around Ferus. He was just glad he was a good enough pilot to keep up with them.

"Not bad for a space pilot," Ditto circled back to yell at him. Ferus could tell he'd earned the boy's respect.

When they were clear of the airspeeders, he signaled Ditto that he was leaving and peeled off toward the spaceport. He dodged the air traffic and zoomed inside the hangar. He abandoned the swoop and activated the ramp on the cruiser. He knew it was only a matter of time before the stormtroopers figured out what had happened.

The ship was empty. He accessed the engine compartment and climbed in. He slid the transpasitor into place and heard it click. Then he ran a quick systems check, careful to set the calibration perfectly. Everything flashed green. He was good to go.

He started up the cruiser and contacted Trever on the comlink at the same time. "Be ready. I'll be there in thirty seconds."

"But I haven't finished my bantha burger."

Ferus grinned. He knew Trever would be ready.

He maneuvered the cruiser out of the hangar and out into the spaceport while he called for clearance at the tower. He headed for the cantina, a large building that was on one side of the landing area so that smaller space cruisers could pull up directly outside. At this slow speed he could see Trever's blue hair and the knot of the resistance leaders huddled around a corner table on the terrace. It was a busy cantina, with beings entering and exiting and table-hopping, and though he couldn't hear the roar and buzz of conversation, he could imagine it.

His comm unit crackled to life, and he heard his registry number.

"Report to control office," an officer commanded.

They had checked on the registry and seen it was temporary.

Ferus activated the comm. "Didn't read that. Heading for departures and will check in with departure agent. Over."

"Check in at control office, over."

"Over," Ferus muttered, shutting down the comm.

He stopped outside the terrace. Trever already had the leaders moving, heading for the cruiser by the back exit. Ferus activated the ramp. The leaders hurried toward him. Ferus was counting seconds now.

The airspeeder patrols came winging over the spaceport. Suddenly the red light flashed near the departure area. They must have traced Ferus here. They'd closed down the spaceport.

Suddenly the messengers appeared from out of the sky, piloting their swoops with seeming recklessness but perfect control. They dived toward the permacrete runways, circled, and spun in tight loops. Ferus saw Laurn's red hair fly and her cap tumble to the ground.

The stormtrooper patrols had to practice evasive action in order not to crash. Other vehicles scrambled to get out of their way. In seconds, the scene was mayhem.

The resistance leaders attracted no notice as they

hurried toward the ship. Everyone else was looking up at the sky.

"Take over," Ferus said to Wil. Wil slid into the cockpit as Ferus leaped out a few meters onto the runway. Ditto flew down, close to him, his hand outstretched. Ferus tossed the bundle of credits high. Ditto snatched it and zoomed away.

The leaders were all aboard now. Ferus hurried back inside the ship and closed the ramp. He took the pilot seat back from Wil.

"Time to get out of here," he told Trever.

He lifted off into the crowded sky. Ditto and the others flanked him for a moment. Ditto gave him a salute.

Ferus zoomed away. He could see the Imperial ships taking off after him. He pushed the engines hard. The craft responded. Within seconds they'd reached the upper atmosphere.

He dived and pushed the speed, hoping to make it past the planet's gravitational pull and into space.

Trever bent over the radar. "We've got ten ships coming up . . . they're splitting into two groups."

"They might not be authorized to leave the planet's atmosphere," Wil said. "But they'll send out an alert galaxy-wide."

They stared out at the Imperial fighters, willing them to turn back.

Ferus pushed the engines. He was close now. He had a fast ship and enough lead time. The fighters couldn't catch him. One by one, they dropped out.

Wil passed a hand over his forehead. "That was a little too close."

Trever grinned. "Ferus always pulls it out."

Next stop was the asteroid. But now their ship was on the Imperial alert list. They had a long way to go.

CHAPTER NINE

Clive and Astri weren't sure of their next move. They had to assume that Toma would be able to reach Ferus. But if they had an idea of where he was, they could track him down themselves. They decided to head to Coruscant and see if they could find Curran and Keets.

They stopped for refueling at a spaceport on a small planet near the Core. They couldn't make it back to Coruscant without refueling, but they didn't like to stop. They chose a limited spaceport with rudimentary services, hoping the security would be as lackluster as their amenities. The spaceport was basically a large landing platform with a line of docking berths on pockmarked permacrete. A tiny cantina without a door was tucked in a corner. A couple of mechanics sat outside, playing sabacc.

Astri looked at the regulations as they flashed on the screen. "I'll have to check in personally over in the control office." She stood.

"If they figure out we stole this ship, you could get arrested. I'll go."

"No, I'll have a better chance to escape notice." Astri tucked a small blaster in her boot. She straightened.

"Leave your comlink open so I can hear what goes on."

She nodded. "If anything goes wrong, leave without me."

Clive glanced at her. She held his gaze.

"I mean it," she said. "No heroics. It's too important to get the information to Ferus."

Should he leave her if they were spotted?

Sure. Too much was at stake.

Would he leave her?

No way.

She waited for him to agree. Clive felt something momentous happen inside him. Something he'd never felt before.

He wasn't going to lie.

"I'm not going to leave you," he said.

"You have to."

"It would be easy for me to say yes," Clive said. "But I'm making a pact with you now. Now, before we begin. I'm not going to start it with a lie."

Astri's face flushed. "Begin what? Our journey?"

"That's not what I mean." He turned his back on her and fiddled with a control. He couldn't say what he meant, or felt. Couldn't say the words. He could only hope that she knew already. If they survived all this, they would be together.

He felt her hesitate behind him. Then she put her hands on the back of his chair. "I know what you mean," she said. "So we'll start out with some rules. We won't lie to each other. And we won't leave each other behind."

He felt her go, a breeze against his neck. He heard her boots thumping down the ramp. Clive smiled. Everything had changed. Everything looked different now. This dusty wreck of a spaceport, the thick orange sky. He had been in this struggle to fight the Imperials because he owed it to his friends, because he owed Ferus his life, because deep down the Empire just ticked him off.

Now he had something else to fight for.

Astri.

She wanted to be annoyed at Clive for distracting her, but Astri felt warmth spread through her as she walked to the control office. She hadn't realized her feelings about Clive had changed so much until he'd spoken. At first she'd disapproved of him, then she'd grudgingly accepted that he wasn't such a bad guy. And then that had shifted into something else. She didn't know what was ahead, but she knew she'd face it with Clive. She had a partner now.

She walked into the office. A junior Imperial officer sat at the desk, looking bored. She wondered what he'd done to get assigned to this outpost in the middle of nowhere.

"Papers?"

She handed over her documents. She pretended to scan the horizon, but she was actually trying to study the data screen in the reflection of the transparisteel. She couldn't read it but she knew from experience that if there was a problem the screen would flash. If that happened, she was prepared to fight her way out.

How far would she go?

Would she shoot this officer? She looked at him more closely now and saw the way he'd tried to comb his hair over his large ears. He was young. Blond stubble glinted on his cheek. She peeked at his insignia. A low-level officer. He could have come from many of the planets in the galaxy that had little resources or wealth. For young people on those kinds of worlds, the Empire was a way out. Lune had told her about some of the young boys and girls at the new Imperial Academy. He'd said for some of them, their good reflexes were the only thing they had. It wasn't so much that they joined the Empire — they just wanted to fly and see the galaxy.

"Not much to look at out there," the officer said.

"You don't seem to get many visitors." She gazed at the reflection. She didn't see anything flash, and the officer didn't change his posture.

"Having trouble with the transmission," he said. "It

can get slow on this planet. Atmospheric haze with ion particles . . . hard on comm systems."

Astri flashed him a smile. He seemed almost human. "So you get to be in the middle of nowhere, and you can't even call out."

"You got that right."

"So, how's the cantina? Will I survive if I have some grub there?" Astri asked. She was beginning to feel nervous. This was taking too long. She could see that Clive had finished refueling.

"You take your chances."

"Listen, what if I just go pick up some food? By the time I come back, my clearance might come through," Astri said. "What do you say? Give a girl a break — I've been living on protein pellets."

He gave a last glance at the screen. "I don't know . . ."

"I'll be back in three minutes. Promise."

"All right." He turned back to the screen.

She walked out and headed toward the cantina. Clive's voice came from her comlink. "Making friends in there?"

"What should we do?"

"Play it out. I can see that the comm system is down."

"But Clive, what if . . ."

He paused. "You do what you have to do. I'll be right behind you. Wait . . . I just got a clear signal . . ."

"I'll go back." Astri hurried toward the control office. When she entered, the officer was just returning to his desk.

"Okay, we're back up to speed." He glanced at the screen and this time Astri didn't have to squint in order to see the flashing alert.

He looked up and his eyes met hers. Time seemed to stop. The moment extended while neither of them moved.

She reached down, took out her blaster, and fired.

One of the things Hydra liked about her job as an Imperial Inquisitor was the attire. She liked feeling enveloped in the robe that swept the floor and the hood that, if worn properly, completely shadowed her face. She had been raised in a tiny hut with a silent, savage uncle, and darkness brought her not comfort, but a sense of where she belonged.

She had been scratching out an existence on her homeworld, serving her uncle and enduring him, when Palpatine had risen to power. She had seen him on the HoloNet news when he declared himself Emperor.

"Just what we need," her uncle had said, and spat on the floor. "Another politician in charge. Nothing to do with us."

But something in Hydra thrilled to it. One person taking on the challenge of ruling a galaxy.

As she cleaned the floor that day, as she herded the

animals the next, as she lay awake in the cold night, it had slowly come upon her that her situation prepared her exactly for this new way the galaxy had turned. She knew how to serve power. She knew both cunning and subservience. Now she could use her skills to serve a better master.

She had left that day. She knew where she belonged.

It had taken her months to find the right way to break in. She had found work, but no opportunity to rise. She wasn't a talker, and she had never learned the art of subtle flattery, advancing your cause by breathing compliments in a dullard's ear. She was only good at watching. And efficiency. She came to see that the Empire valued efficiency more than anything else. And that was what would transform the galaxy, she was sure. Efficiency would streamline travel and communication and industry, and the galaxy would be a beautiful thing, running like an enormous BRT computer, a humming majesty of a thing.

Her efficiency was noticed finally. Lord Vader put her on the Inquisitor's team and checked in with her, making sure she was advancing and receiving important assignments. That had puzzled her, because one of the things she admired about him was that he didn't seem to be the type to care about those things. Then she realized that he had placed her there for another reason. It was simple: He wanted her to tell him what the other Inquisitors were doing, who was close to Sano Sauro, and if any assignments came from the Emperor himself.

Hydra was pleased to do this. Lord Vader was next to the Emperor. It gave her a thrill to be valued by someone so powerful. When she was made Head Inquisitor she obtained her reward. Her first reward. She knew there would be more to come.

This was the first time he'd given her an important assignment. Of course she had reported to him on Ferus Olin's activities, but that had just involved keeping her eyes and ears open. She hadn't come up with much. And her work on Alderaan hadn't pleased the Emperor. Hydra had felt her status slide, and it had made her sick inside. She couldn't fail at this job. She had nowhere else to go.

But now Lord Vader had asked her to do something that was obviously important. If she did well, no doubt he would pass along word of her prowess to the Emperor.

Then I might have need of you, he had said. Hydra thrilled to the memory of it.

The comm unit signaled, and she answered it. She was in luck. The ship had been spotted. It had been snared in a routine stop that was starting to be instituted in the Core. Imperial ships would pick a quadrant and order all ships to report to a nearby space station. There they would wait in rows until their registries and papers were checked. It was a massive inconvenience for so many, but it showed everyone who was in charge.

Apparently a mechanic on an out-of-the-way space-port had sent out a message. The ship had filed false registry numbers and had taken off without clearance. It was just luck that it had been caught in the snare.

No, not luck, Hydra thought. *Efficiency.* Put enough controls on gateways in the galaxy and you were bound to catch what you were looking for.

She was close to the space station. She ordered the official to detain the ship. She would be there soon to arrest its passengers.

CHAPTER TEN

"So what do you think will happen to the ship after we complete the mission?" Trever asked Ferus. They were alone in the cockpit. The ship was now in hyperspace, safe for now.

"Good question," Ferus said. "We should probably talk about that at the meeting. We have two fast, new ships. We can decide who needs them most."

"I've already decided," Trever said.

Ferus laughed. "Ah, let me guess. Would that be you?"

"Hey, I'm in the resistance. And I need a ship. Therefore . . ." Trever shrugged. "C'mon, Ferus, let's take this one. It's such a sweet ride. These sublight engines really crank. I know we had a little engine trouble, but once we get down there and really get a look at her, we can tweak her. Put in an extra ion drive for a backup system and we'll be golden."

"The used parts dealer told me that these new engines sometimes have problems with the transpasitors and magnetic fields," Ferus said. "It seemed like he was telling the truth — wait a second." Suddenly he bounded out of his chair. In a moment he'd accessed the engine panel and climbed down.

"Going to check?" Trever asked. "Good idea. Do you need a glow-lamp down there?"

Trever heard Ferus grunt, as if he were trying to use some muscle to loosen a part.

"Need a hand?"

Ferus reappeared, hauling himself up and then sitting on the floor of the cockpit. "We have a problem. There's a tracer beacon on the ship. When the parts dealer mentioned a magnetic storm, it didn't make sense. Then I remembered that sometimes tracer beacons have a small magnetic field. If it's placed close to a transpasitor, it could affect it."

"An *activated* tracer beacon?" Trever couldn't wrap his mind around it. "But how can that be? Do you think it's some sort of security system that the salesman back on Coruscant didn't get a chance to dismantle?"

Ferus shook his head. "I wish it were so."

"But that means . . ."

"There's a spy somewhere in our group."

"But that's impossible!" Trever said. "Everyone on this ship is a resistance fighter."

"I know. But someone on the ship is a spy."

They didn't say anything for a moment, just stared at each other. Ferus went over the process in his head. Over the past twenty-six hours they'd traveled to three spaceports and picked up twenty-one resistance leaders. He had always been in the cockpit where the engine compartment was located, or Trever had. Except for their unscheduled stop. That was the only time the cockpit had been empty.

"While I was out looking for the part, did you notice anyone go into the cockpit?"

Trever thought carefully. "We were all in the salon most of the time. But then when we were getting ready to move to the cantina, someone could have sneaked in. I didn't keep track of everyone. I didn't know . . ."

"It's all right, Trever. You had no reason to suspect anyone."

"What are we going to do now?"

"Well, the tracer can't work steadily in hyperspace, so we're all right for the moment. As soon as we leave hyperspace, we've got to contact Ry-Gaul and Solace and arrange a meeting together before we get to the asteroid. We need to go over all the ships before we proceed. We can't assume that the other ships are clear. We can't bring a spy to the asteroid, so we either have to cancel the meeting or figure out who it is. And we have to do all this fast before we put the whole group in danger. The future of the galactic rebellion is on these three ships."

Ferus jumped to his feet and went to the nav computer. "We need someplace close to the asteroid, but not too close. Not a spaceport. Not a planet . . ."

"A moon," Trever said.

"An uninhabited moon." Ferus flipped through the possibilities quickly as the star map hologram flashed. He reached out a finger and pointed. "Here. XT987. Now let's just hope that Solace and Ry-Gaul are within range."

After he reverted to normal space, Ferus contacted Ry-Gaul and Solace and was relieved when both responded. Now he had the hard task of informing the resistance leaders that they would have to land. Ferus presented it as a necessary step before proceeding to the base, but there were grumbles and some dissent.

"Every stop we make puts us in danger," Boar pointed out.

The fractures in the group were widening. This was a group who had risked everything to resist the Empire, but they each had their own ideas. They were too used to danger and uncertainty to panic, but they weren't happy.

Ferus was glad to see Ry-Gaul's ship and Flame's cruiser already waiting when he arrived. This meeting would have to be quick. There was no telling where the

Imperial forces were at this point, only that they were monitoring his progress across the galaxy. A short stop wouldn't cause much alarm; something prolonged might cause them to investigate.

He signaled to Ry-Gaul, Solace, and Flame to join him. "We've got trouble," he said. "I'm sure there is an informer aboard my ship. There's a tracer beacon planted in my ship's engine. I put a trace scrambler on it for now. It'll fool whoever is tracing us, but not for long."

Ry-Gaul didn't react. He never did. Solace narrowed her eyes, and Flame looked shocked. "That's impossible," she said. "They are all heroes."

"So we thought," Ferus said.

Solace shook her head. "This means the Empire knows about Moonstrike."

"It doesn't matter if they know," Ferus said. "It only matters if they find out who's involved. None of the members knew each other before this trip."

"What was the time frame when you were away from the cockpit?" Ry-Gaul asked. "Do you have any idea who did it?"

Ferus shook his head. "That's the problem. I can't narrow it down."

"We can't let this derail the meeting," Flame said. "I promised them all safe passage." She clasped her hands together. "This is a disaster!"

"Well, we can't lead them to the asteroid," Solace said. "That's clear. Ry-Gaul, let's check our ships just to be sure." Ry-Gaul nodded shortly. To Ferus, it seemed that Ry-Gaul had something he wanted to say, but he wasn't ready to say it. He resolved to ask him privately.

Solace and Ry-Gaul went off to check the ships. Flame turned to Ferus. "Who do you think it is?" she asked. "You must have some suspicions."

"I don't," Ferus said. "Boar Benu has been argumentative . . . suspicious of everything I do. It could be a way to throw suspicion off of him."

Flame nodded slowly. "He was in an Imperial jail for a time. They could have gotten to him there."

"That's not a reason to suspect him," Ferus said. "I've been in an Imperial jail. Twice."

"If Ry-Gaul and Solace find that their ships are clear, maybe we should load all the members — minus the ones you were ferrying — onto one ship," Flame suggested. "Give me the coordinates and I'll take them to the asteroid. The Jedi can remain and set up a trap."

"It's not a bad plan, but let's wait and see what Ry-Gaul and Solace propose," Ferus said.

Ry-Gaul and Solace returned. "My ship is clean," Solace reported.

"Mine, too," Ry-Gaul said.

"Flame proposes that she take most of the group on until we figure out who the spy is," Ferus said.

"We've come this far," Flame said. "We can't stop now."

"I think one of us should take my ship and lead them on a wild goose chase," Ferus said. "That will buy us time."

"Ry-Gaul, maybe you should do that," Solace said. "You can leave the ship on an out-of-the-way planet, with the tracer beacon activated. Then Flame will take the resistance leader and pick you up and proceed onward. But first, we have to trap the spy."

Ry-Gaul spoke for the first time. "The leaders must be getting restless. Solace, Flame, why don't you see if you can calm them down."

The two went off to the other two ships. Ferus turned to Ry-Gaul. "Ask Solace to be a diplomat? You've got to be kidding."

"I wanted to talk to you alone." Ry-Gaul's silver eyes stayed on Flame as she walked away. "You are assuming the tracer was placed aboard while you were off finding the new part," Ry-Gaul began.

"That was the only time I left the cockpit," Ferus said.

"You are making an assumption."

Ferus thought for a moment. It took him several seconds to catch up to Ry-Gaul. "I'm assuming that the tracer was placed *after* we got the ship. But we could have obtained the ship with the tracer already on board and activated."

Ry-Gaul didn't say a word. He let Ferus work it out.

"But that would mean that the Empire knew we

would take the ship. And the only way they would know that would be . . ." Ferus felt his breath catch. "If Flame was an Imperial spy."

"It is a possibility we should not overlook," Ry-Gaul said. "She was the one who set us up with the ships. It almost seemed too easy, if you think about it."

Ferus felt a surprising rage gather from the soles of his boots to the top of his head. He was tired of maybes and uncertainty. He was furious that they were at this crossroads. They were at the mercy of one person who was holding up the completion of an intricate plan. He felt the anger grow, and this time he didn't turn away from it. The Sith Holocron whispered something to him that made sense.

Let your anger go. It's time. When you are thwarted, use your anger.

"There's one way to find out who it is," Ferus said. "Line them all up. Threaten to kill them all if one of them doesn't confess to being the spy."

Ry-Gaul looked startled. Ferus realized that the thought in his head had come out. It was one of those thoughts he didn't understand, the ones that didn't seem to come from him. Ry-Gaul focused on him, really examining him in a way that made Ferus furious. How could he not know that anger was a weapon like any other?

Because the Jedi are weak.

That's why we destroyed them so easily.

They never saw it coming.

Ferus stalked away. He put his hands on the Holocron. He was finally ready. Here on this uninhabited moon, in the middle of the galaxy, in the middle of uncertainty.

Hidden behind the ship, he slipped the Sith Holocron out of his tunic and set it in motion. Images came at him, a rush of knowledge that seemed to be absorbed before it was registered. Terrible things, fascinating things, things that made his stomach churn. He didn't know how long he looked; it felt like hours. He had to wrest himself away. It took all of his strength.

It had only been seconds.

He blinked. He had seen too much to process, but he knew he had been changed. He felt the Emperor's hand on him now.

Ry-Gaul was suddenly in front of him. "I felt something . . . the dark side of the Force. Ferus?"

He gathered himself together. He mustn't let Ry-Gaul know. He turned to face the older Jedi. He saw the careworn, silver eyes, the stubble of silver hair. Ry-Gaul suddenly looked pathetic to him, not strong.

"Ferus?" Ry-Gaul narrowed his eyes.

"The spy is Flame. You're right." He had been given a glimpse into dark hearts, and he recognized the breed. Facts clicked in his head, motivations, cunning.

Ry-Gaul strode forward suddenly and grabbed him by the shoulders. "Forget about the spy. I feel the dark side of the Force. Not from Flame, my friend. *You.*"

"Tell me something," Ferus answered. "What is so wrong with using anger? 'Feel your anger, let it go,'" he mimicked. "What did that philosophy do for the Jedi? What did it get us but . . . here?" He waved his arms to take in the bleak, rocky moon, the ships, the evidence of their being hunted, the evidence of their exile.

Ry-Gaul dropped his hands. "The Jedi made many mistakes. We were . . . fooled."

"*Fooled?* Children are fooled! The Jedi lost the galaxy!"

"The galaxy was not ours to lose."

"They destroyed us, and we never saw it coming!"

"Ferus." Ry-Gaul spoke his name with anguish. "To act with anger as your propulsion is never the way."

"It is the only way. It is the only thing we have left!" Ferus took a step backward. "I will not be taken down. I will not be hunted. I'm going to take care of this now."

He stalked away. He could feel Ry-Gaul behind him. Close. Too close. Afraid of what he might do.

He found Flame standing with Solace and Trever, their heads together, discussing their next move.

"It's Flame," Ferus said. Why bother with preliminaries? "She's the spy."

Solace didn't show her surprise. She looked to Ry-Gaul for confirmation.

Trever shook his head. "You're crazy, Ferus. What are you talking about? She arranged this whole thing. She started Moonstrike."

"Exactly," Ferus said. "What better way to cut off the effective resistance movements at the start than by getting them in one place and destroying them?"

"You don't have much to say, Flame," Solace said.

"I don't think Ferus would listen," she said. "I think the accusation is ridiculous, of course. I've been fighting with you, shoulder to shoulder. I was shot on Bellassa rescuing Amie Antin."

"That's right, Ferus!" Trever said.

"Yes, you got a blaster wound during the operation," Ferus said. "You must have been furious. You didn't know the full extent of the plan, only that we were going to rescue Amie. It was a perfect way to prove your loyalty to the Eleven. You needed Wil and Amie to commit to Moonstrike, and it was the only way to ensure that they would join."

"Tell them about Rosha, Trever," Flame said. Her voice was steady.

"She brought us through heavy fire," Trever said. "She risked her life to save the Roshan delegation. And she put the ship down and offered to go out first, to make sure it was safe. I went with her . . ."

"And Imperial fighters appeared and blew up the ship before the Roshans could exit," Ferus said.

"That wasn't her fault! There were no fighters on the sensor screen! And she stayed with me and helped me on Rosha, even while the whole capital city was burning. She found us food, and shelter, and kept us safe. And then she found the resistance and got together with them —" Trever faltered.

"Yes, she found the resistance, didn't she?" Ferus encouraged. "She brought them together, maybe even helped set it up. Only it worked a little too well, didn't it? The Roshans turned out to put up an amazing fight, a fight no one had expected, and Vader didn't want another Bellassa on his hands. So she called a meeting and told the Empire where it would be —"

"But she was there, too! We were all caught when they blew up the building! She saved my life," Trever said desperately. "She pulled me into a crawlspace underneath the floor."

"Things go wrong sometimes," Ferus said. "The order to attack is given a few seconds early. No doubt she'd planned to be out of there before it happened. Leaving you, most likely."

"No." Trever shook his head stubbornly.

"Trever, don't you see?" It was all so clear to Ferus now. He knew the way Vader thought. And he had no doubt that Vader was running this operation. "She is always in the midst of the battle but is never killed. She brought them all in and promised them safety and recruited us. All this time, she was drawing us in. How do you think the Empire found out about Thugger's Alley?"

"No," Trever whispered. He shook his head again, more vehemently than before. "She couldn't have."

"That was part of Twilight. The operation we couldn't figure out. It is one strike against all the most powerful resistance leaders at the same time. He will crush the rebellion before it has a chance to start! And he used Flame to do it."

Solace's comlink signaled, and she stepped away. She listened for a few minutes.

When she returned, her face was grave. "That was Clive and Astri. They've been on Flame's trail for some time now. Clive suspected her. They've discovered her real name. Eve Yarrow. She's an Imperial agent."

Flame's face darkened. "It's not true!" Now at last her manner began to crack. "Liars!"

"What should we do now?" Solace asked quietly.

Ferus felt a surge of power. The Sith Holocron burned his skin, but he enjoyed the sensation of burning. He felt a darkness around him, a shimmering, beautiful thing.

"Execute her," he said.

CHAPTER ELEVEN

"At least we got through to Ferus about Eve," Clive said.

"What did Solace say?" Astri kept her eyes on the nav screen. They had been pulled into a routine check by Imperial vessels and were lined up on a spaceport runway. Imperial starfighters buzzed overhead, making sure no one took off.

It was a tense situation, but they had prepared for it. At the last spaceport Clive had used Imperial equipment to key in a new ID profile and registry.

"Who, Lady Chatty? Nothing. She just said, 'I understand,' and broke the communication. She was with Ferus and Flame, though, so Flame is caught, no question. The question is, what do we do now?"

"Vader mentioned the Bespin system," Astri said. "We could head out there and see what we can find out."

"That's a long way to go just to noodle around," Clive said. "We don't have any clear information to go on. We still don't know what Twilight is." He watched Astri's face. He was beginning to be able to read it. "Don't blame yourself for what happened at the space-port," he said. "You couldn't shoot him. That's a good thing. And we got away."

"It was a failure of nerve," Astri said. "I could have compromised everything. I had my blaster aimed at him. But I couldn't fire directly at him."

"Maybe we're not cut out to be spies. Look, we can fight the Empire with everything we have, but we don't have to turn into them."

Astri stared at the nav screen but she was picturing the scene back at the spaceport. The Imperial officer, looking at her. She, pointing her blaster at him. All she could see was his eyes, young and afraid.

She'd moved the blaster just a couple of millimeters and blasted his computer instead. The officer had sprung back, fumbling for his blaster, and she'd moved for-ward quickly and placed her blaster against his head. "The next one is for you if you move," she'd said. She put all her will into the words, but she'd known they were hollow.

Then Clive had arrived. They'd taken the officer's blaster and comlink, and had destroyed the rest of the communication equipment. It bought them time. But they knew that the next ship to land would give him access to a comm system.

"We're already wanted for stealing the cruiser," Clive

said as they left the planet. "So now we'll be wanted twice. Destroying an Imperial computer system should get us a couple of years in jail, no question."

Astri wished she knew how far she was willing to go to be a resistance fighter. She knew she wasn't willing to kill. No, Clive was right. She didn't want to turn into them. She didn't want to lose sight of who she was.

She stared at the screen, waiting for their number to be called up and given a release. No ships had taken off in some time. "Something's wrong," she said. "The line should be moving faster than this."

"Let me check it out," Clive said. He lowered the ramp and exited the craft, then ambled off toward a knot of spacers talking in a group.

"What's going on, mates?" he asked. "Anybody know what the holdup is?"

A short, pudgy pilot in a greasy flight suit snorted. "You think they tell us anything?"

"What I don't get is, they've checked ships through that they're holding on the ground," another spacer said. "You'd think they'd release them."

"Or let us park in the hangar and wait this out in the cantina," a spindly pilot broke in.

"I'll tell you what this is, if you ask me," the second spacer said. "I've seen this before. They're holding us all here because they're waiting for some Imperial topper to get here. Mark my words, they want to arrest somebody, but there's nobody here important enough to do the job."

"So we've got to broil under these three suns while we wait for some topper?" The pudgy pilot blew out a breath of air in exasperation. "I've got a cargo hold full of premium dates from Nantuker that're spoiling as we're talking. This is one long blasted twilight of a day, let me tell you."

Clive ambled away, not letting his pace reveal his worry. He checked out the Imperial officials at the control office. They certainly didn't look too busy. They were waiting. In the small cluster of buildings was a detainment center, a fancy word for jail. He hoped he wouldn't find himself in it.

He scooted back up the ramp and told Astri the news. "I'm afraid the people they're waiting to arrest are us," he said. "We've got to think of a plan."

"It's a space station," Astri said. "We've got nowhere to go. And look at all those TIE fighters lined up. We can't outrun them."

An Imperial ship appeared in the sky. It swept down and landed in front of the line of space vehicles.

"This is not good," Astri said as a hooded figure emerged. "It's an Inquisitor."

"I'll place bets that it's Hydra," Clive said. "She fits Ferus's description."

"She knows we're here," Astri said.

"There's only one way out of here," Clive said. "That's aboard her ship."

"Steal an Inquisitor's ship?" Astri asked. "How are we going to do that?"

"Carefully," Clive replied.

The spaceport was thrown into a moderate amount of confusion due to the presence of an upper-level official. Officers flocked to the command center, trying to impress her. Low-level functionaries laid low, trying to escape notice. And the spacers, pilots, cargo drivers, and freighter captains were furious that they were being held up this long. They began to complain. Loudly.

The pilots and passengers were out on the permacrete runways now, milling and discussing the holdup. It was easy for Clive and Astri to thread through the crowd unnoticed, even as a voice over the loudspeaker ordered everyone to return to their vehicles.

Hydra had put down her craft directly in front of a bulk freighter that was outfitted for passengers. The crowd was confused and angry, and it gave Clive and Astri cover to quickly board Hydra's ship. She'd left the ramp down in her haste.

"What's your plan?" Astri asked, peering out the viewport. Stormtroopers with blaster rifles were beginning to get the crowd under control. Clive and Astri didn't have much time. "I know you have a plan. I just hope it doesn't involve taking off with about fifty TIE fighters shooting at us."

"We're going to sail out of here like a free bird." Clive hurried to the small stateroom. He flung open a small recessed door.

"You see? Even an Inquisitor needs a change of clothes." He flung an Inquisitor's robe toward Astri. "Put this on."

She looked at it. "You've got to be kidding."

"I don't kid when I'm looking at prison time, kiddo."

Astri donned the robe and pulled the hood forward. She was the same height and size as Hydra, and Clive thought she had a good chance of pulling this off.

"Give me five minutes to get arrested," he said. "I'll be wearing a hidden transmitter . . . let's hope they don't find it. Hydra isn't going to let these officers get credit for the arrest. She's going to want to interrogate me. She'll take me into that detainment cell. When I'm alone with her, wait a few minutes and then come into the main office and tell them to let you into the cell."

"What if she doesn't take you into the detainment cell? What if she takes you aboard the ship?"

"Then we hold her hostage and escape that way."

"Great," Astri muttered. "Just great."

Clive started out the ship, then stuck his head back in. "And may the Force be with you," he said with a quick grin.

He vaulted out of the ship. Astri pressed close to the viewport. She watched him walk toward the control office as though he didn't have a care in the world.

She heard his voice come through the transmitter. He asked when he'd be able to take off. Then she heard boots clicking and Clive saying, "Whoa, mate, no need for that, I'll just wait for my turn . . ."

And a voice, low and clear. "Arrest him."

"Arrest him," Astri said out loud, trying to match that voice.

Clive narrated his arrest so she'd know where he was. "Where are you taking me? I haven't done anything. Hey, everybody flies under a false registry sometimes. My cruiser wasn't up to inspection, so I . . . aw, not a detention cell. This is cruel."

Astri heard the unmistakable sound of security locks snapping. Then Hydra's voice again.

"Who were you with at the Dexus-12 spaceport?"

"No one. I was alone."

"Correction. You were with a woman. What happened to her?"

"She left me. Women always do."

"What were you doing on Niro 11?" Hydra asked.

"Banking," Clive answered. "Isn't that the only thing to do on Niro 11?"

"If you refuse to answer you'll encounter more persuasive techniques when you meet Lord Vader."

"I did answer, Your Inquisitiveness," Clive said. "Next question?"

Astri checked her reflection in the durasteel door. She walked down the ramp and headed for the control office. Underneath the cover of the long sleeves of the robe, she crossed her fingers.

She strode into the control office. The officer at the console looked surprised. "Inquisitor Hydra, I thought you were with the prisoner."

"I'm returning there now. Give me the security device for the cell."

"That's against procedure. The prisoner could get it from you."

"Correction. I am Head Inquisitor, captain. Nobody gets anything from me." Astri put out her hand. After a moment's hesitation, the officer put the security device in it.

"That will unlock the cell," the office informed her. "If you need me, there's a comm unit near the door with an emergency call button."

She nodded and turned away.

She walked through the connecting hallway to the detainment cell door. Outside the door she stopped for a moment. A locked cabinet contained a few blaster rifles, stun cuffs, and a stun net launcher. She coded in the number she saw on the door onto her security device. The cabinet opened. Astri grabbed the stun net launcher. Then she pressed the button to release the locking device of the cell and walked in.

Hydra had her back to the door. "I said I didn't want to be disturbed."

Astri put a blaster against her back. "So sorry."

She reached around and took Hydra's blaster from her utility belt.

"Do you mind?" Clive gestured toward his stun cuffs. Astri pointed the security device and released the locking mechanism.

Hydra gave a small, chilling smile. "You won't get away with this."

Astri activated the stun net launcher. The stun net wrapped around Hydra, forcing her to the floor and imprisoning her, unable to move or speak.

"Correction," Astri said. "We *are* getting away with it."

"We'd love to stay and chat, but you don't seem to be in the mood for talking," Clive took Astri's hand and squeezed. "Ready to take me prisoner, my beauty?"

Astri gestured with her blaster. "Get in front and I'll march you out."

She unlocked the detainment cell door, and they slipped out . . . but not before Clive rigged it so nobody would be using the door anytime soon.

Astri kept her blaster on Clive. She marched him out to the outer office.

"I'm taking the prisoner to Lord Vader," Astri said. "Institute full clearances for my ship."

"Right away."

Astri felt sweat snake down her sides as she marched Clive toward the ship. At every step she expected to be called back. But they made the ramp and climbed aboard. She threw herself into the pilot seat and started the pre-flight check.

Clive kept his gaze out the viewport. "So far, so good. Aren't you going to compliment my genius?"

"We're not gone yet." Astri spoke into the comm, "Clearance requested."

"Clearance granted."

She pushed the engines, and the cruiser shot into the air. They left the spaceport behind.

"Okay," Astri said. "It was a genius plan."

Clive settled back into the copilot's seat. "Better late than never."

CHAPTER TWELVE

Ferus saw the Jedi turn to him in astonishment. He didn't care. He felt as though he were looking at them from a distance.

Trever's eyes . . . He couldn't quite meet Trever's eyes.

"You can't!" Flame's voice was shrill. "You can't just . . . do that!"

The resistance leaders, tired of waiting and knowing something bad was going on, had climbed out of the cruisers, and now surrounded Flame and the Jedi in a tight knot.

"She is an Imperial spy?"

"This is outrageous!"

"You promised us safety!"

"We *are* safe," Solace said sharply. "So let's focus on what to do next."

"Ferus Olin is right." Boar spoke up. "I don't countenance this, but we have no choice. She can identify all of us. There's too much at stake. We must execute her."

"Wait." Flame licked her lips. "We can bargain."

"We don't make bargains with traitors!" one of the leaders said.

"There is a backup device aboard my ship," Flame said. "It will lead the Empire to you if you don't dismantle it. Trust me, you won't find it. Only I know where it is. It is tracking you right now."

"It could be a trick," someone said.

"All right," Ferus said. "We give you your life if you dismantle the device."

Flame nodded nervously. Followed closely by the others, she headed toward her ship.

"Did you mean that?" Trever asked Ferus.

Ferus wasn't sure. The voice inside him said, *Why should you keep your word?*

"Ferus, the dark side is working on you," Ry-Gaul said. "Solace and I can feel it. You must tell us what's happening to you. You've been a double agent for too long. Has the Emperor given you something to hold for him?"

"No." *No, I am holding it for me.*

"You said you would execute her," Ry-Gaul continued. "That is not the Jedi way. If you are struggling, let us know."

"Don't think we can't understand," Solace said. "We've wandered the galaxy since Order 66. We've seen and done plenty. I was a bounty hunter, remember?"

"We both drifted away from the Force and came back again," Ry-Gaul said. "Just connect with the Force. It will show you the path. Just connect."

Ferus saw compassion in their eyes, not worry. Some of the veil lifted from him. He felt himself coming back. He felt the Force flowing from Ry-Gaul and Solace.

He was spared from answering when Flame returned with the others.

"She did it," Boar said. "There was a device hidden in the cargo hold. Impossible to find, as she said. So now we must spare her life."

"We'll leave you here with survival equipment," Solace said. "This moon isn't so far out of the way. There are plans to map this quadrant. Someone will find you eventually."

"You're really going to leave me here?" Flame asked. "I can't be here alone! Trever, don't let them!"

Trever turned away.

The three Jedi walked toward the ships. "Solace had a good idea," Ry-Gaul said. "I'll take Ferus's ship and activate the tracer beacon. I'll leave it at a crowded spaceport and transfer to Solace's ship. Then we can head for the asteroid."

Ferus felt his head clear. The distance between him and the others didn't feel as wide. He drew strength from the living Force he could feel in Ry-Gaul and

Solace. He shook his head, trying to remain with them, all of him, his heart and mind. He tried to grasp the knowledge he felt he'd gained without letting it suck him in. He had seen into the mind of a Sith, and he felt he knew better how it worked.

"Vader will have a backup," he said. "Not just the one on Flame's ship. He would have something else, some other way to track us. Solace, you told us that Clive said Vader was heading to an emergency drop. I think Flame left Vader a message there. She is only acting afraid now. She knows Vader will find her. I have to get to that message before he does. So don't go to the asteroid until you receive the all clear from me."

"But how do you know where the secret drop is?" Trever asked.

"The Bespin system?" Solace asked doubtfully. "That's an awfully big place."

Ferus shook his head. "The place has to be more central than that. She wouldn't have had time to get to Bespin and back to Coruscant to leave him a message. I have an idea."

"I want to come with you," Trever said.

Ferus hesitated. Part of him didn't want Trever with him. He couldn't forget the look on Trever's face when he thought Ferus would execute Flame. If he had to access the dark side of the Force again, he didn't want Trever to see it.

Still, he couldn't think of a reason to refuse. And part of him, the part that was still a Jedi, wanted Trever with him. Maybe if he went too far, Trever could save him from himself.

He nodded shortly.

"Where are we going, anyway?" Trever asked.

"Back to Coruscant."

They said their good-byes. Ferus could see the worry in Ry-Gaul's and Solace's eyes when he took his leave. He turned his back on them, not wanting to see it there.

Then he turned again. He didn't want to leave them this way. Their gazes still rested on him.

"I won't fail you," he said. "You must trust me."

"Trust in the Force," Ry-Gaul said. "It will hold you. Connect."

In deep space, stars burned and fell. Trever felt as though the future was rushing toward him. Whatever was going to happen seemed inevitable. It seemed he couldn't turn away. He was bound to accompany Ferus, no matter where he was going. No matter what he would do.

Looking at Ferus's face, he felt the difference in him. It wasn't just that the humor was missing. Something that used to flow between them now was stopped up. It came through at odd times, odd moments. Trever wished he could take Ferus by the shoulders and shake the old Ferus out of him again.

"So are you going to fill me in?" Trever asked. "Where's the secret drop?"

"Do you remember that day you told me you saw the ruined Temple, and how sad it made you feel?" Ferus asked.

Trever nodded. "Now that I know Jedi, it's the ultimate new moon bummer."

"You saw Flame that day, too."

"That's right. She was surprised to see me. She'd just been to see Bail Organa, she said. Or she sorta said it."

"Bail Organa was on his way to Alderaan that morning," Ferus said. "He might have been there already."

"After Dex's hideout was raided . . . when I thought everyone was dead . . . Ry-Gaul and I saw her sitting in a café. When she saw us, she said how relieved she was. But . . . when I think about it, I don't remember relief. Only surprise." Trever felt the strain in his voice. "Do you think she meant for me to die that day?"

"I think it's possible. Certainly the raid was meant to hit Ry-Gaul. Flame had no way of knowing the two of you were rescuing Linna Naltree."

"So do you think the secret drop is at the Temple?" Trever asked. "Why?"

Ferus spun in his chair to face Trever. The ship was on autpilot now. "There was a fellow student at the Temple when I was there. I knew him well, though we weren't friends. One of his favorite places to retreat to was the Map Room. Everyone knew that about him."

"Okay," Trever said. "But the Temple is destroyed. And what does that have to do with Vader?"

"The Map Room is still intact," Ferus said. "I saw it when we broke into the Temple. And that Padawan became a great Jedi. And then he became Darth Vader."

"You mean you knew Vader when he was young?"

Ferus nodded. "Now that I know that, I know other things about him. Things I can use."

"Whoa, let's revert to normal speed. You're going too fast for me. Are you saying you're going to fight him again?"

Instead of answering, Ferus turned back to the instrument panel. "Right now I'm focusing on keeping Moonstrike on track. The best revenge would be to turn this all around. Start a rebellion from a snare the Empire created to destroy one."

Trever settled back into his seat with an ease he didn't feel. "Back there, on that moon . . . when we found out that Flame was an Imperial agent . . . you said to execute her because you were trying to pressure her. I mean, you wouldn't have *done* it, right?"

Ferus turned away, not answering. He heard the question as a rhythm in his blood. What would he do, how far would he go?

Could he have killed Flame?

Was this what happened to you, Anakin? Did you feel yourself splitting? Did the faces of those you cared about seem to be talking to you from a distance? Did you feel your anger growing, and did it feel good to have it grow? Did you think you were right . . . and they were standing in your way?

Did you hear a Sith's voice in your head and think it was yours?

CHAPTER THIRTEEN

The ruined Temple filled his vision. Ferus felt oddly calm. It had started here, his life's journey. He had come here as a baby. He had left here as a young man, sick at heart. He had returned to find everything he'd loved had been destroyed.

And now here he was again. He could feel the Force here as though it was carried on the wind. But the wind was part of the Force, as much as the clouds and the sun and the millions of beings who inhabited this planet. He mustn't forget that. He mustn't only see corruption and decay. That was what the Emperor wanted him to see.

"I want to go in with you."

"No, Trever. I'm going alone." Ferus didn't even lean on the words. There was no way he was bringing Trever into danger.

At least I can spare him this.

"The security isn't as tight now that the Empire isn't using the Temple," he said. "I'll go in, see if I'm right, see if there's a message. Then I'm out." He turned to Trever. "No arguments. Just wait here for me."

He left Trever and circled around to the base of the Temple. He saw the crumbling stone of the ruined terraces. There — just above him — what once had been transparisteel had been shattered. Plastoid had been adhered to the opening as a clumsy fix, but there was room there to sneak in. With the help of a lightsaber.

The plastoid peeled back silently. He slipped inside. He knew where he was immediately. The Temple was part of him, every chamber, every hallway.

He stood in the center of the ruined room. For a moment he allowed himself the luxury of remembering. The breakfast room. A smaller, more intimate space where sometimes the Padawans were allowed to share the morning meal with the Jedi Masters who were in residence. It was chosen for its morning light, of course. And the light — Ferus closed his eyes, remembering. As thick and golden as the butter on their plates, streaming in to warm fingers still cold from the chill of morning exercises. On fine days the transparisteel rose into the ceilings and the room became filled with fresh air.

He remembered his fingers curling around a thick mug of steaming tea. The smells of thick slices of bread fried in sweet butter and syrup. Fruit heaped on serving plates. The Jedi Masters, relaxed in this setting, smiling at their students. And the day ahead, filled with study and activity, with meditation, with play.

This was what they had destroyed.

He walked through, cinders crunching under his boots.

Outside in the hallway he turned a corner and found himself in the grand atrium, stories high. The huge windows were boarded over. The stones were blackened and pitted. Still, as different as it was, he knew the way, even in the darkness.

He walked softly, making no sound. He could feel no trace of the Living Force here. He allowed his anger to build, let it rest inside his chest. He could pull it out when he needed it. The Emperor had taught him that.

The turbolifts had been shut down, so he had to climb the staircase that curved through one of the spires, all the way up to the Map Room. The walls were half-destroyed. The floor was uneven, with deep holes blasted out of the stone. Ferus looked into one and saw the floor of the atrium hundreds of meters below. Yet when he waved his hand over the sensor the holographic map of the galaxy sprang to life.

Anakin had sat in here for hours sometimes. They'd all known it, and they'd all left him alone. He had the ability to send whole systems spinning, memorize details of language, atmosphere, minerals, history, geography . . . and then send another system spinning, then another, then another and another and another . . . and keep all the facts in his head, and remember them.

He had been so gifted.

The Chosen One.

Ferus walked through the holographic maps, through curtains of information, schematics, words and images. Pale blue, red, gold, green . . . the whole galaxy whirled around his head. He walked through the display to the Bespin system. He accessed the planet with its gaseous atmosphere.

Facts appeared: language, geography, chemical properties. He touched the thick gas cloud with his finger. The message appeared.

No coordinates on asteroid. Tracer beacon installed on two ships. Three ships total. Will be on comm silence. Emergency beacon in boot. Will activate if needed.

And then the blinking coordinates of where Flame waited. He'd been right. She'd had one last trick up her sleeve. Knowing Vader would come here and see where she was. He erased the coordinates.

His worst fear — that somehow she had discovered the location of the asteroid, had passed it along — was unfounded. The meeting could proceed.

He shut down the system.

Vader hadn't been here yet. He'd beaten him here. Vader would have erased the message.

Ferus took the stairway back down to the main level, curving around the spire until he reached the main floor. He walked out into the grand hallway, his hand on his comlink, ready to send the message to Solace.

He felt him an instant before he saw him, striding

down the center hall, as though the Temple was still standing as it had been, as if what surrounded him was still noble, still beautiful. His boots rang on the pitted, blackened stone. He walked as though he owned the Temple.

He thinks he does *own it.*

Vader saw him.

They stopped. From one end of the vast hallway, full of echoes of the past, they faced each other.

CHAPTER FOURTEEN

Solace lurked on the edges of the atmospheric storm. It was a good place to hide. Gravity shifts were tossing small asteroids about like stones from a child's hand. It wasn't nearly as bad as it would be once she flew into the center of the storm, but it kept things interesting while they waited. Ry-Gaul sat in the copilot seat. They'd left Ferus's ship at a planet in the Mid Rim. She hoped the Imperial forces were heading there now.

Things were coming to a close. She had joined Ferus reluctantly. After her colony on the surface of Coruscant had been raided, she'd felt no more purpose in her life. Ferus had offered her a cause, and that had been irresistible. After Order 66, she had vowed never to trust again. Yet Ferus had drawn her in. It had felt familiar to fall into this group, heroes in her mind, Dex Jettster, Curran, Keets, Oryon, and of course Trever. Not so much participating — she wasn't much of a talker — as simply being.

Now their objective had been reached. They had a hand in the beginning of a rebellion. Solace felt sure that Ferus would have a new challenge after this one.

Ferus. She was worried about him, and she didn't like to worry about anyone. Ferus had lost something. His work as a double agent had compromised him. Both she and Ry-Gaul could feel it. She hoped he would find his way back again.

The emergency channel flashed. Solace leaned forward, her heart racing, and accessed the comm unit. It was Toma.

"Ferus got a message out. He gave the all clear. You can bring in the resistance leaders. Stormtracker says the storm will increase in intensity in a few hours. Enough to break up a ship. Come immediately."

"Copy that," Solace said. "Leaving now."

She walked back to the stateroom, crowded with the passengers. They looked up expectantly, their expressions calm. They'd been through plenty already. They knew how to wait.

"We got the all clear. I'm flying into the storm. Things are going to get rough," she said. "Use the harnesses to strap yourselves into the chairs. You'll need them, I guarantee you. But don't worry. We'll get through. Unless we go into complete systems failure. But that's a pretty remote possibility."

She saw some of them pale. One of the leaders strapped his harness tighter.

Solace went back to the cockpit to study the storm-tracker map. She was glad she was flying Flame's ship. It was fast and agile, yet solidly constructed.

Although the gravity shifts and massive asteroid showers made for seeming chaos, it was helpful to note patterns before going in. In the most intense parts of the storm, it was hard to have even an instant to check a navigational aid.

"So I heard what you said," Ry-Gaul. "You mentioned systems failure."

She shrugged. "I said chances are it won't happen. But the ship is about to meet some powerful forces. I was trying to reassure them about their options."

"That was your idea of reassurance?"

She magnified the stormtracker so it would be easier to check during the journey.

"Let's go," she said.

The storm always began with sudden air pockets and increased meteor activity. This was when pilots would rethink their idea of shaving off some mileage by flying through part of the storm. This is when they resigned themselves to a new flight plan and a delayed arrival to wherever they were going.

Solace set a course for the heart of the storm.

The air pockets turned deep and wicked. It was inevitable that the ship would hit them; they were impossible to avoid. They sucked the wind from you and slammed you against the seat.

The gravity shifts almost tore the controls from her hands. She could avoid the biggest asteroids but occasionally one would pass close enough to knock the ship off course. She was hanging on to the controls now, her hands clenched into position, her eyes straining to see every detail in the vast swirling grayness.

"Asteroid, port side!" Ry-Gaul said, his voice tight. She evaded it by meters.

She threaded her way through an asteroid field and dropped into an air pocket so terrifyingly deep she actually heard shouts of fear from the lounge. She zoomed out of the pocket and went into a screaming dive to avoid another one. Tiny asteroids peppered the shields of the ship. The controls shuddered under her hands.

The storm was worsening. Solace fought to keep the ship steady. Auroras shimmered ahead, deep purple and orange. Their glow lit up the cockpit.

She was drenched in sweat and casting an uneasy eye at the systems controls when Ry-Gaul said, "The asteroid is just ahead."

She took a chance and pushed to maximum speed. She outran a rocketing asteroid and zoomed toward a satellite of rock so large it had its own atmosphere.

Immediately, the ship smoothed out . . . slightly. The ride was still bumpy, but she felt in control.

She landed near the small cluster of duraplastoid survival domes that comprised the base. Toma and Raina emerged from one of the shelters and came toward her.

Lune came running, followed by a slower Garen Muln. Oryon brought up the rear.

The resistance leaders filed out on shaky legs, gazing up at the odd yellow sky, the air currents whipping around fully visible.

"Welcome to our base," Toma said. "Let the first Moonstrike meeting begin."

CHAPTER FIFTEEN

Ferus saw the glow of Vader's lightsaber as he activated his own.

This was it, then. The final confrontation.

He was ready. His rage was ice and fire.

He charged.

His first blow was easily parried. He came at Vader again. Again. Circling, jumping, vaulting past him, turning. Each time his lightsaber came toward him, it was either deflected in a shock that ran up his arm, or . . . Vader simply wasn't there.

"If you cannot even touch me, how can you win?" Darth Vader asked.

Ferus focused on his anger. He remembered Palpatine's words.

There is no limit to what you can do.

He charged at the dark figure again. This time his strike came close. He touched the edge of Vader's cape. He smelled the singed material.

Now, while he's off balance. Now.

"Maybe I'll just get lucky," Ferus said. *"Anakin."*

Vader came at him with surprising swiftness, but Ferus was able to Force-leap away. Still he sensed that Vader was holding himself back, playing with him for now.

"So you know who I was," Vader said. "Do you think that would make a difference to me? Anakin Skywalker is dead."

"Was it because the Council wouldn't let you become a Master? You always had to struggle with your ego, didn't you?"

"It was never a struggle. I was always the best."

" 'Best' is not a Jedi concept."

"That is the trouble with the Jedi."

Ferus wasn't tired yet, but he knew he was expending too much energy. He was tapping into his anger and fighting better than he ever had, but it wasn't enough. He had to unsettle Vader. He had to find the key.

He had everything he needed to defeat him, didn't he? He had the Sith Holocron for strength, Vader's true identity in his hand, his own rage. With those tools, he could do it. The Emperor had told him he could. Ferus thought quickly. He wanted to pick the battleground. Someplace that would unsettle the former Jedi.

There — the stairway to the Jedi High Council spire. Ferus started to climb. He knew Vader would follow.

He came out into the circular room. It was half rubble, the seating blackened lumps, the vast transparisteel shattered. Wind whipped through the room.

The Dark Lord entered. The wind blew back his cape. He stood, legs apart, ready for battle. Looking forward to it, Ferus was sure.

"The Emperor cannot protect you now," Vader said.

What next? What could Ferus do to get him off balance? He suddenly had a flash of intuition. He remembered what Keets had told him.

"What about Senator Amidala?" he asked, leaping away from Vader. He faced him, his lightsaber held in an offensive position. "What about Padmé? What happened on Mustafar?"

He felt the quake in Vader. He had reached him at last.

"Do not mention her name!"

"I thought it was a lie, that the Jedi killed her," Ferus suddenly understood, the Sith Holocron burning under his tunic. "It wasn't. You killed her, didn't you? You killed the woman you loved."

Vader's wrath filled the room. Ferus could feel it. Instead of turning away from it, he *took* it. He filled himself with it.

This is what the Emperor meant. This is the last step.

He flew across the room and this time he landed a blow.

Vader roared. It was a howl of fury, inarticulate,

undisciplined. Totally unlike his usual icy control. The control box on his chest started to smoke.

Stones in the floor ripped out and were flung toward Ferus. He dodged them, rolling and twisting away. A blackened piece of furniture flew across the chamber and smashed into the wall over his head.

Anything that could be torn from the floor or walls came at him — conduits, debris, hunks of stone. He dodged and weaved, attacking and retreating as Vader hit him with everything he had.

"How did you kill her, Anakin? Did you lose control? Did you see her die, Anakin? Is that why you wanted Zan Arbor to perfect that drug? Was it for you, Anakin? So you could forget her? So you could forget *your wife*?"

Another roar from Vader. Part of the ceiling gave way. Durasteel melted, smoke rose from the debris. Ferus leaped over a gaping hole in the floor and attacked Vader again, but his lightsaber cut through empty air.

The anger inside Ferus was now like liquid fuel inside him. He was feeding off Vader's rage, he was pushing every molecule of his body and feeling every molecule of the room respond to him. Everything was clear, hard-edged. His body obeyed him without any hesitation, and his mind was focused. He had no doubt that he could defeat Vader. No doubt.

And *that* was what the dark side brought him.

When he won, when he defeated him, he could take the victory to the Emperor, and he could be greater than Darth Vader, more powerful than even the Chosen One had been.

He charged at Vader and made contact. Vader waited a beat too long to deflect him. The blow shuddered off his body armor. Something inside fused and the plastoid melted. Ferus could smell burning circuits. At the same time, he detected a tremor in Vader's arm.

Suddenly he was picked up and slammed against the wall. He fought to hold onto his consciousness.

"Don't . . . get . . . cocky," Vader said.

Ferus rolled away from the blow that followed, barely escaping. He looked up. For a moment Vader was just a shape at the side of the room. For a moment, a trick of the eye or the light, he saw the room as it had been. The seats were restored, the air traffic outside flashing, the potent energy of the Force filling the room because the Jedi Masters were still alive.

Ferus felt it invade him, the sense of peace and light.

No, push it away! Listen to us! You could have been a great Jedi Knight, and they let you go! They never appreciated you!

It was true, wasn't it? Ferus saw himself as a Padawan, standing before the Masters. Taking responsibility for something that wasn't his fault. Tru's lightsaber. He had fixed it secretly. . . .

He remembered that day. He remembered the compassion in that room.

Another vision came to him, of himself as a Padawan, accepting responsibility for what he had done. The Jedi Masters sorrowful, showing him the two paths he could take. He could have stayed. He chose to go.

His choice.

The room returned to its ruined state. He was crouching, breathing hard.

Connect.

The Force was still here in the ancient stones. The stories of all the Jedi who had lived and died here, they were here, too. His story was here. Not as distinguished as most, shorter than many, but his. He had followed the path for as long as he could, as well as he could, and the Masters had never asked for more than that.

He felt the wisdom of the Masters inside him, and he gripped that feeling with his hands and let it fill his heart. He rose. He had no doubt that they had reached out and touched him. Many hands on his shoulder, showing him. Here is one way. Here is another. Choose.

He had come so close.

He walked out of the dark side and into the light.

I am a Jedi.

Now he knew with absolute certainty that he had to be rid of the Sith Holocron. It had been slowly poisoning him. He had been a fool to think he could take what he wanted and not be corrupted. He had fallen into the Emperor's trap. Almost.

He Force-leaped over Vader, surprising him, and let himself fall into the hole in the floor. He heard Vader's chuckle.

"Run like the coward you are!"

The wind whistled past his ears as he fell. He landed safely in the Map Room. He headed for the stairs.

He took each turning at top speed, Force-leaping most of the way. He knew where to go. The heart of the building, the power core. No longer operational, it would still contain enough residual energy, if not to destroy the Sith Holocron, then to damage it. He ran through the hallways and found the central conduit that ran, he knew, straight down to the power core. He reached into his tunic.

You are throwing away your only chance at success.

This is not the kind of success I want.

The voices of darkness were a clamor inside him as he held the Sith Holocron. He threw it in. He felt something rip inside him. It was an agonizing pain that sent him down on his knees. He breathed through it, calling on the Force to help him.

He felt it lift. He was exhausted, but he was free. He was himself again.

Vader came out of nowhere, raising a gloved hand. Ferus felt himself lifted up, over Vader's head. He couldn't breathe.

"You should know before you die that your dream is dead," Vader said. "Don't you know I can bow *anyone* to my will?"

Ferus was slammed against the wall. He felt himself losing consciousness.

He was glad, in the end, that he would die here at the Temple. With the ghosts of his friends, his mentors, his fellow Jedi. He would become one with the Force in the place he first discovered and nourished it.

CHAPTER SIXTEEN

All in all it wasn't a bad start, Raina observed. The resistance leaders hadn't yet acquired the kinds of layers of protocol that bogged down the leaders of planets. They actually listened to each other. They could get things done.

The Roshans and the Samarians were talking about sharing technology that might result in a super droid that could take on Imperial weapons technology. The leader from Naboo had a suggestion about how to sway politicians to join them. They all soberly discussed Tobin Gantor's report, delivered by Oryon, which stated that the Empire might be working on a super weapon. The discussions were fast and lively. Raina suddenly felt that Moonstrike might work after all.

Toma had told her to stay and act as a kind of moderator in order to control disputes. But she was in a funny position here. She was part of the resistance, but she didn't represent her homeworld. The others had discussed

Flame — or Eve Yarrow — at the beginning of the meeting. Raina felt ashamed, even though she'd had nothing to do with Flame's betrayal. Flame came from Acherin.

She walked out onto the rocky ground. Overhead, the sky was darkening. Toma had said the storm was intensifying. When that happened, it would often be so dark on the asteroid that you couldn't see your hand in front of your face.

She could see the shadow of Toma through the plastoid of the communications dome. She went toward it. The wind was picking up, and she couldn't hear the sound of her own footsteps. She thought ahead to the evening meal. She had hoped to set up glow-lamps to eat outside but with this wind it would be impossible.

She stopped in the doorway, waiting for her eyes to adjust to the light. Toma was bent over the console. She walked closer. He didn't turn, intent on his job.

At first she couldn't make sense of what she was seeing. But she'd been a top-ranked pilot on Acherin, and she knew how a homing beacon worked.

"What are you doing?"

Her voice startled him. He turned, surprise on his face. Surprise and unease. "Raina! I thought I told you to stay in the conference dome."

"Answer my question." Disquiet ticked inside her. "That's a homing beacon."

"It's for Ferus. You know he can't find us without it."

"That's not our coded channel."

"Raina . . ."

"Toma, what's going on?"

He said nothing.

Her voice was a whisper of disbelief. "Are you . . . a traitor?"

"No," he said fiercely. "How can I be a traitor to something that doesn't exist?" He leaned forward, spitting out the words. "What are we doing here, Raina? What did we commit to? A dream from a man who had once been a Jedi as a boy. He left us here for months to babysit his dream."

"We *offered*."

"He should never have accepted our offer. He knew what it would mean. While he was chasing nonexistent Jedi, I almost died here!"

"That was the risk you took when you pledged your support to him! He couldn't have predicted your illness. He brought more supplies as soon as he could."

"And what did I get in return? The Empire has won, Raina, and we have to accept it. It's the only way we'll get our homeworld back. It is torn apart by civil war."

"And the Empire is allowing it to die!"

"It's our fault! The Acherins are fighting each other now. They'll destroy Acherin — there will be nothing left if we don't act now. They need a leader, someone who will restore the government and take the reins. Someone who will have the backing he needs to institute reforms, fix the infrastructure."

She fell back against the table. "By the light of the ancients, I don't believe it. They've offered you the chance to rule Acherin, and you betrayed us for it."

"Come with me," Toma urged. "We can return to Acherin together. We are old friends, Raina. The best of friends. We fought side by side. Together we can save our homeworld. Eve Yarrow will return as well, and with her we can do anything."

"Turn off that homing beacon, Toma."

"No, you don't understand —"

"No," she said, drawing her blaster. "*You* don't understand."

"You wouldn't kill me."

"I will do anything to protect this base."

She had made a mistake, she saw, when he half-turned. She'd thought he was unarmed. He had a blaster up his sleeve.

The bolt hit her in the heart. She fired, and he staggered and fell.

Raina's legs wouldn't work properly. She was telling them to move, and they were failing her. She tried to reach the homing beacon but everything was so dark. She stumbled forward, felt herself falling, but it was like falling into a cloud. She felt nothing now.

When she hit the hard ground it was as though she had jumped into her childhood bed on Acherin, the one piled with her mother's quilts, where she had played at night in the close darkness, pretending to be a pilot, pretending to be a queen, waiting impatiently to grow up and do something — anything — that would prove her courage.

CHAPTER SEVENTEEN

Outside the Temple, Trever sent out the distress call, and they all responded. Keets, Curran, Clive and Astri, who had just landed on Coruscant, and even Malory Lands. All they had to hear was that Ferus was in trouble, and they were there.

They found Ferus in the great hallway.

They gathered around him. Trever sank to his knees. His disbelief and his grief burned his chest. "No," he cried.

Astri knelt by Ferus and touched his hair gently. She dropped her head in her hands.

"Wait." Malory hovered over Ferus, taking his vitals. "He's not dead. Not yet, anyway." She went to work with her diagnostic tools. "He needs a bacta bath, but I'll have to treat him here, for now."

Trever stepped back as Malory prepared her medications. She worked over Ferus for long minutes while they waited.

Finally they heard him groan.

Malory leaned back. "He's coming around. Don't try to talk, Ferus."

"Vader . . ."

"He's gone."

Ferus tried to sit. Malory pushed him down. "Don't move."

"He's on his way there . . . to the asteroid. He said he could get to anyone."

"He's confused," Malory said.

"No, he's not," Trever said as he bent down and looked into Ferus's eyes. "He's himself again. What is it, Ferus?"

"Warn them . . ." Ferus sat up. "Tell them not to go."

Trever shook his head, his eyes wide. "They are there already."

"I have to get there."

"You can't go anywhere! You need complete bacta immersion." Malory tried to gently push him down again, but with a surprising show of strength, Ferus stopped her hand.

"What is it?" Trever asked.

Ferus looked at Clive and Astri. "Vader said something about awakening a mole. Remember? But Flame . . . was an active agent from the beginning. He always has backup, remember? Someone on the base has betrayed us. I'm the only one who can stop him. I need the Force to stop him."

"But . . ." Trever said.

"Don't worry," Ferus told him. "I have it back again."

Trever was worried about Ferus. His face was drawn and white, and he looked like he was about to keel over. He had insisted on taking over the pilot seat as soon as the ship neared the asteroid. Luckily the fast-moving storm had moved close to the Core, and they were able to reach it quickly.

"Keep trying to get Solace and Ry-Gaul at the base," Ferus said. He kept consulting the stormtracker. "I don't like the looks of this," he muttered.

"The storm's interfering with the comm system, that's for sure," Trever said. "Wait — I'm getting some breaks here. I think I've got an open line!"

A holo-image of Ry-Gaul appeared. "I'm here. The meeting is going well."

"Ry-Gaul, we have a problem," Ferus said quickly. "There's a mole at the base. Someone. And Vader is on his way. You must evacuate everyone. Do you copy?"

"Copy that. The storm is growing — I don't know if —"

The image fractured into particles of light.

"At least he heard you," Trever said. "They'll be able to get out before Vader arrives."

"I hope so." Ferus leaned back and closed his eyes. His skin was white against his dark hair. "I hope so."

* * *

Ry-Gaul, Garen, and Solace bent over Raina and Toma. They had both fallen millimeters from each other.

"Toma fired first," Solace said.

Ry-Gaul turned off the channel on the homing device. "Toma was the mole."

"I can't imagine why he turned," Garen said. "I never suspected him. Not for a moment."

Ry-Gaul shook his head. "There's no telling how close Vader is."

"We'd better rally the others," Solace said. "There's no time to waste."

"We'll need to destroy the equipment before we evacuate," Ry-Gaul said. "There might be data on the computers that could help the Empire."

Wil had come with them, anxious to help. "I'll do the pre-flight check and get everything ready," he said.

"I'll get Lune," Garen said.

Ry-Gaul began to set explosives in the dome. They would blow it when they were airborne. He looked out the plastoid viewport to Flame's ship. Wil was doing the pre-flight check.

It was lucky the ship was still in shape to get them out of here.

Get them out of here. . . .

Vader never leaves anything to chance. He always has a backup.

Ry-Gaul raced out of the dome. He could see Wil behind the cockpit viewport, ready to start the engines.

"No!" he shouted.

He ran toward the ship at top speed.

The explosion hit him in the face, and he felt himself blown backward. He landed on the ground, looking at the burning ship. The cockpit had been completely destroyed. He tasted smoke and dust.

Solace came up and helped him to rise. They stood silent for a moment as grief filled their hearts.

"Wil Asani," she said. "We lost one of the best."

The resistance leaders ran out of the dome.

"What's happening?" one of them shouted. The group stood well away from the heat of the burning ship.

Solace kicked the dirt with her boot. "Vader had no use of Flame anymore, so he rigged her ship. She would have blown herself up. Most likely the plan was for her to leave before the air attack."

"We have no way off now."

"We'll have to make a stand here. We have some surface-to-air weaponry. We might be able to hold out until Ferus arrives."

Ry-Gaul was staring up at the sky. "Do you remember the talk of the superweapon that Tobin Gantor was working on?"

"You think it can destroy an asteroid of this size?"

"I do."

Solace swallowed. "If that's true, we can't tell them."

"No. If it's going to happen, it's better that they not know."

The flames were dying down on the ship. Solace looked over at it. "There's no way that ship will ever be flown again." She looked closer. "Ry-Gaul, look. The port side doesn't have too much damage. Isn't that where the escape pod is?"

"Let's take a look."

Ry-Gaul walked over with Solace. Garen joined them, leaning on the cane with the repulsorlift motor that Toma had made for him.

"The escape pod isn't damaged," Ry-Gaul said. He checked the instrumentation.

"Looks like a miracle," Garen said. "It'll fly."

"And there is only room for one," Ry-Gaul said.

The three Jedi looked at each other. They said the same name at the same time.

"Lune."

CHAPTER EIGHTEEN

Trever looked at the stormtracker and gulped. The storm was the worst he'd ever seen, and that was saying something. He had gotten more used to flying in and out of the massive storm, but he'd never done it in this kind of intensity.

He looked over at Ferus, who was gathering himself, studying the stormtracker intently. His tunic was wet with perspiration.

"Are you sure you can do this?" Trever asked.

Ferus turned to him. His eyes held the light Trever remembered, like a beacon in a dark velvet night. "The Force will see us through," he said. "Try to raise the base one more time. I'd like to know what we're going to find before we go in."

Trever turned back to the comm unit. He tried again to reach Ry-Gaul or Solace. "It's out."

"Then we go in. Strap yourself in." Ferus activated his own harness.

He pushed the engines and drove straight into the storm. He went far faster than he usually did. He had reconnected to the Force at the Temple, and he felt stronger. His body was failing, but the Force would take him through. He had no doubt about that.

The ship shuddered as it was slammed by a vortex. It spun until Ferus regained control. Ferus dived as a huge asteroid shot by. It left a space-wake behind that buffeted the ship. Trever was nearly thrown out of his seat.

The severe magnetic shifts were creating vibrant auroras of light — beautiful to see but tricky to navigate as they obscured the small asteroids that barreled unpredictably through the storm.

"Asteroid field to starboard!" Trever rapped out. The ship lurched as Ferus corrected.

The ship suddenly shifted into a deep pocket and plummeted. Ferus felt the terrifying drop in his stomach but let the ship go, knowing that if he fought it, it could break up the vessel. When he felt the pocket ease, he brought the ship back slowly, turning with the vortex until he found a hole in the pressure and shot through it into bumpy space.

"Stars and planets, Ferus!" Trever's face was white. "That was close."

Ferus veered around a medium-sized asteroid. He hugged it for a short time, staying in its draft. It was large enough to leave a small gravitational pull that Ferus could use to steady the ship. The only trick was staying close without slamming into it. Its path was erratic, and it turned and lurched from side to side. Ferus didn't look at the instrument panel. He reached out to the Force, letting it tell him what would happen before it happened.

"Ferus . . ."

"It's all right, Trever. We can hug this for awhile, let it take us closer."

"No. Ahead. I thought it was an asteroid. But it's not."

Ferus had to lean close and peer through the atmospheric haze. Through the shimmer of a purple aurora, he saw a dark shape.

"It's an Imperial Star Destroyer," he said. "It's Vader."

"A Star Destroyer? He's in a Star Destroyer?" Trever's voice went high and thin. "That is not good news. He could have hundreds of starfighters in that thing."

"I doubt it. He's probably running with a small crew. He won't think he'll need that much support. We can't outrun him. We just have to hope we can beat him there and evacuate the others."

"We can't outrun a Star Destroyer!"

"Don't tell me we can't, Trever. Just watch out for asteroids."

Ferus kept in the draft of the asteroid. The good news was that even a Star Destroyer's magnetic systems would be inoperable. He wouldn't pick up Ferus's ship on radar.

His only advantage, as Ferus saw it, was that he knew

what the asteroid looked like. He'd been to the secret base enough times that he could pick out the asteroid from space. To someone else, it would look like any other. And he hoped Ry-Gaul had dismantled the homing beacon. Vader would have general coordinates, but he wouldn't know the exact spot of the base.

The asteroid suddenly plummeted into a space pocket. Ferus had anticipated it a half-second before and had already compensated by zooming up, out of range of the gravitational pull. The ship was slammed and rocked back and forth but he held steady.

They were close. Far ahead, Ferus could see the telltale cloud around the asteroid base. He checked the position of the Star Destroyer. His only hope was that Vader would pass the asteroid by.

"There's a ship on the radar," Solace told Ry-Gaul in a low tone. "I got a clear view before it went out. It looks like a Star Destroyer."

Ry-Gaul nodded. He crouched down next to Lune. "Are you ready?"

The boy shook his head. "I don't want to leave you."

Ry-Gaul put his hands on his shoulders. "You know you must, though, don't you? Your mother needs you. The galaxy needs you, too. You must grow up and be safe."

Lune nodded, his gray eyes intent on Ry-Gaul's face.

Garen crouched next to him. "Remember all I taught you. The Force will protect you."

"Trust the Force, not your instruments, to get you through the storm," Solace said. "Once you're through, the nav computer will be operational. Find the closest spaceport and land. Find someone you can trust to help you get back to Coruscant."

Lune never cried, but now his face was tight with the effort to hold in his tears. "It's not right to leave your friends."

"Yes, it is," Garen said. "You are our hope, Lune. We are sending you off."

"May the Force be with you," Ry-Gaul said. "Remember what we taught you, and trust yourself."

"Courage," Solace told him. It was strange. Here, at the end, she had finally found words of reassurance. "We know you can do this."

Lune entered the escape pod.

The Jedi stood together, shoulder to shoulder. Overhead the skies roiled with thick atmosphere, clouds colliding against clouds, but they knew the storm was lessening in intensity.

"We had a good journey in this life," Ry-Gaul said. "I'm ready to join the Force."

"The galaxy will find its balance again," Garen said. "It won't need us to do it."

"I am happy to be standing here with you," Solace said.

* * *

Everything had worked out so well, Darth Vader thought.

Ferus Olin was dead. Or close to it. Close enough to die slowly on the Temple floor, to suffer as *he* had suffered on Mustafar.

And now he was in the perfect position to test the first prototype of the superweapon by blasting Ferus's dream — and the beginnings of a rebellion — into space dust.

He didn't need the homing beacon. He had already locked on to the coordinates. He had pushed those scientists on Despayre to come up with a program to estimate size, weight, and gravitational pull based on a homing beacon. He could target the asteroid without trouble.

And there it was ahead, spinning in a gaseous cloud.

"Set coordinates," Vader told the crew.

"Set."

"Lock on."

"Locked."

"Fire."

Trever screamed.

The energy bolt had been huge. It had hit the asteroid dead center.

One minute it was there, spinning ahead of them. Then there was nothing but debris.

The blowback from the explosion was so huge that it

hit the ship and knocked it backward. The ship bucked and rolled. Ferus fought to bring it under control, while his brain frantically tried to make sense of what his eyes had just seen.

The base was gone.

Somewhere he heard Trever keening. "No, no, no, no . . ."

Ry-Gaul.

Solace.

Garen.

Oryon.

Lune.

The leaders of the resistance on dozens of planets. He felt the loss of so many lives as a great pain inside him. The Living Force receded like a wave that knocked him off his feet.

Red lights flashed. Cockpit alarms sounded.

"We're going into systems failure!" Trever yelled.

Ferus fought to save the ship. He reached out to the Force. He had to gain control because he had to follow Darth Vader. He had to follow him because he needed to be stopped, and Ferus had to find a way to do it.

It was as though Ry-Gaul spoke in his ear.

"Look."

He looked. A small arc of light, too faint for a star, a trajectory of speed.

An escape pod.

"Lune," Ferus breathed.

He fought the dying ship. He eased it into a current that was somehow stable. It was like a gift handed to him by his friends.

The Star Destroyer sailed through the debris cloud, heading off to escape the storm.

He had a moment of calm to consider. Two choices.

Follow the escape pod.

Follow Vader.

His anger was one path. Hope was another.

He chose.

CHAPTER NINETEEN

The sandstorm had been blowing for two weeks straight. The nights were freakishly cold, the mornings bitter. With no suns to bake it away, the cold had seeped into the hut. The sound of the sand peppering the walls and the howl of the wind could drive you mad if you were inclined that way.

Obi-Wan Kenobi knew that this storm, like all things, would pass soon enough. Until then, he lived with grit. Sand was in his food, in his bedding, in his hair.

Anakin had always hated sand. Now Obi-Wan knew why.

He didn't hear the knock over the sound of the wind, but he sensed a presence outside his door. Obi-Wan opened it a crack. Ferus stood, bearded now, the sand thick in his hair, his eyes almost shut by the dirt and sand caking his eyelids. Obi-Wan pulled him inside and shut the door.

He saw at once that Ferus couldn't speak. The Living

Force was weak in him. Obi-Wan led him to the sleep couch and left him there. He hurried to get supplies.

He bathed Ferus's face in warm water, gently releasing the hardened sand. He kept going back and forth to the cistern for more water and rags. He checked him for wounds and administered bacta. It was obvious he'd been in a fight. There was a large contusion on his forehead, another at the back of his skull.

But that wasn't what had dimmed the Force in him.

Ferus looked at him. His eyes filled with tears. He closed his eyes and turned his face to the wall.

He slept for three days.

Ferus awoke at midnight on the third day. Obi-Wan heard him stirring and went down to the pantry, where a pot of stew had been waiting. He warmed it, then scooped it into a bowl made of thick pottery to keep its contents warm. He poured water from the cistern into a jug and brought it all upstairs on a small tray.

Ferus had risen to a sitting position. Obi-Wan placed the tray on his lap. Ferus shook his head.

"You made it to my doorstep," Obi-Wan said. "You must have wanted to live."

Ferus ate.

When the bowl and the jug were empty Obi-Wan removed them. He sat facing Ferus, waiting.

The words poured out. Vader. Twilight. Ry-Gaul, Garen, Solace — everyone he'd meant to save. Toma and betrayal. Flame. An asteroid the size of a planet disappearing before his eyes. How everything had turned to dust. How Obi-Wan had warned him, and he had ignored the warnings.

How it was all his fault.

"I know it's not the Jedi way to say that," Ferus said, the bitterness and defeat in his voice causing Obi-Wan pain. "But I *am* responsible. I *was* blind. I thought I could defeat Vader — that was driving me always, and that destructive impulse blinded me to things I should have known."

"You had a Sith Holocron working on you," Obi-Wan said. "There are not many Jedi who could resist those voices. The greatest of us have been brought down. But at the right moment you recognized it."

"I was too late."

"You saved Lune. You chose the right path. You followed the escape pod. You brought him back to Astri."

"You don't understand. That isn't enough to save me. I don't know how to go on. In the cave on Illum — I saw visions. I saw a fireball that consumed Garen. I should have known!"

"The visions were not of the future, but of your own fears."

"I saw Siri and she warned me. She said I hadn't lost my arrogance. That I only thought I'd changed!"

"Your own fears, again."

"But Obi-Wan." Ferus's voice was hoarse, his eyes haunted. "What I saw was *true*."

"These things didn't happen because of your failures, Ferus. They happened because *someone did them*. Darth Vader is responsible for those deaths. Not you. He is the one who fashioned the plan to kill. He is the one who blew up that asteroid."

Obi-Wan sat quietly with Ferus for long minutes. He remembered his own bitterness, his own shame and despair. *What had saved him? How could he save Ferus?*

"Forgiveness isn't a feeling," Obi-Wan said finally. "It's a decision you have to make for yourself every day. Every day, you will fight for a moment of peace."

"That is a journey I'm not inclined to take." Ferus leaned back, exhausted. "Everyone I love is dead."

"Not everyone."

Ferus thought of Trever. "No. Not everyone."

"One day you will have peace, Ferus," Obi-Wan said. "Until then I'll give you the only thing I can give you."

Ferus opened his eyes. Obi-Wan's gaze was gentle. Obi-Wan had made it through his own despair. He knew the way. "What is that?"

He had expected gentle wisdom, or maybe a Jedi lesson. Instead, Obi-Wan spoke in a brisk, practical voice.

"A job."

CHAPTER TWENTY

Everything was ready for his departure. His ship was fueled and standing by at the hangar near the Orange District. Keets and Curran had come to say good-bye. Dex was with them, once again in his repulsorlift chair. He had lost weight during his illness and was half the size he used to be.

"Wherever you're going, go safe and be well, my friend," Dex said. He patted him on the back with all four arms.

"If you need us, we'll be there," Keets said.

"We're going a hundred levels down," Curran said. "We found a neighborhood like the Orange District."

"Except it's not orange," Keets said. "Never liked the color, anyway. We found a colony of Erased. They set up in an abandoned field of gigantic cisterns, the ones that used to supply water to Galactic City. They filled them up with water. It's like living on a water world. We're going to live on a house raft. Not bad."

"We won't forget them," Curran said. "Solace, Ry-Gaul, Oryon, Garen, Raina. Heroes all."

"We'll be ready to fight when the time comes," Keets said.

Dex leaned in to speak to Ferus for a moment. "Never believed in second-guessing, you know. You did your best, and that is always good enough. We'll see more losses than these before we're through. They were all great heroes, but more will step up to take their places."

The Svivreni never said good-bye. With sorrow in his eyes, Curran gave the traditional farewell of his homeworld. "The journey begins, so go."

Curran, Keets, and Dex climbed back into their battered airspeeder. Ferus watched until the vehicle blended in with the space traffic and he could no longer distinguish it.

He turned away and began to walk. There was one more thing to do. And it was the hardest thing of all.

Trever sat waiting with Malory Lands. They had use of the clinic for twenty minutes only; Malory had arranged it.

Ferus's steps faltered. Out of all the things he had had to do over the past months, this seemed the most impossible.

He and Obi-Wan had discussed it. Trever had been with them from the beginning. He had heard that Vader was a Sith Lord. He knew the Emperor was a Sith. That knowledge could put him in great danger.

Ferus had a way to protect him.

Malory took him aside. "I've been working on the formula since you gave it to me. I can pinpoint Trever's memories pretty precisely."

"I want him to remember his parents. His childhood," Ferus said.

"He will. But . . ." Malory hesitated. "You understand, don't you, that if I wipe out the last year . . . he might not remember you? His memories will be spotty starting from the death of his father and brother. It will intersect with when he knew you and Roan."

It felt like a great pain was ripping him apart. To remove Roan from another memory felt like another death.

And he would lose Trever, too.

Ferus swallowed. "I know."

"I explained it all to Trever. He's waiting to talk to you."

Ferus approached the boy. He sat next to him on the examining table.

"So I guess this is good-bye," Trever said. "Maybe. You know, the worst part is that I won't remember what a great hero I was. I never thought I could be a hero."

"You'll have your chance to be a hero again. And I'll always remember you as one."

"I was pretty full-moon awesome, it's true."

Malory came up behind them. "It's time. The proce-dure will take at least twenty minutes, so . . ."

"I'll wait at the hangar."

Ferus and Trever slid off the table. Ferus turned to Trever and embraced him.

"I lied before." Trever's voice was muffled. "The worst part will be forgetting you."

There had been times in the past days when Ferus had wondered if he still had a heart. Now he knew he did. He felt blinded by his pain.

"You are my best friend," Ferus said. "That will never change."

He stepped back. He looked at Trever, wanting to remember the affection in the boy's gaze. Then he walked away. He opened the clinic door.

"Don't forget me!" Trever called after him.

Ferus hesitated, then walked out, letting the door close softly behind him.

Vader stood with Lord Sidious in his Master's pri-vate quarters above his office. His briefing had been short and satisfactory. Twilight had been a success. The resistance movement was dead. The preliminary test for the superweapon had proved that one day it would per-form as they expected.

Ferus Olin was dead. Or gone. It hardly mattered.

He had done it all, everything his Master wanted, and more.

"The success of the first stage of the superweapon pleases me," Lord Sidious said. "What does not please me is that you failed my test."

Vader was surprised. "I don't understand, Master. I annihilated the resistance. I destroyed Ferus Olin. He was not our ally. He was our enemy."

"Of course he was our enemy," Lord Sidious said. "And of course I meant for you to destroy him. That was not your test."

"My test . . ."

"You fought him with emotion. Just in the way you pressured Zan Arbor to come up with that memory agent. Yes, I know about that, how badly you wanted it. I had hoped for more from you, my apprentice. I expected you to leave Anakin Skywalker behind. By your actions you have shown me that Anakin is not dead. Until he is dead, Lord Vader cannot truly rise."

A rebuke instead of praise. Instead of a reward, a warning.

"You killed her. That was good — it brought you to me."

You killed her. That was good. Vader was shocked at the grief and anger that roiled through him at his Master's words. He could easily have struck his Master down.

Lord Sidious smiled. "You see?" he taunted.

His Master was right. Anakin wasn't dead. If Anakin were truly dead, he would not be feeling this despair.

"You must accept this — all steps are necessary

when the outcome is this." Lord Sidious raised one arm and took in Coruscant glittering around them, the stars and planets burning above. "The galaxy is in our grasp," he rasped.

"I will eliminate Anakin, Master. And . . . her." He would bend his mind to it. He would banish Padmé without a drug. He would do it with his anger. With his will.

With all that he'd done, with all that was behind him, where else would he go, what else could he do, but this?

He bowed his obedience.

His Master's pale gaze traveled beyond him to the dark night sky. "See that you do. Because until that day, no matter how useful you are to me, you will be a failure."

Astri and Clive arrived in the ship Dex had procured for them. "We arranged for a house on Bellazura," Astri told Ferus. "It's near the beach, so you can see the water. It has a garden. We have ID docs, and credits . . ." Her voice trailed off. "We'll raise him with Lune. He'll have a brother again. And parents . . . We'll take care of him."

"I know he'll have the best possible life," Ferus said.

"Even with me as a father?" Clive tried to joke.

"Well, except for that part," Ferus said.

Astri slung an arm around Clive. "He'll make a great father. He just doesn't know it yet."

"Malory is telling him that he was in an accident," Clive said. "That it wiped away parts of his memory, including the fact that we adopted him. She says that he won't remember us, but with constant contact he might associate us with good feelings in his past."

Ferus nodded.

A med airspeeder approached and landed. Trever climbed out, looking around as though he hadn't seen the hangar before. Malory looked across the hangar at Ferus and nodded. The experiment had been successful.

Ferus watched Trever cross the hangar. He felt his breath catch. Trever's walk was different. He'd forgotten that Trever had been a different person six months before. He'd been a street thief. Over his time with Ferus, Trever had lost that cockiness, that defensiveness. Now it was all there in his walk.

Get your hero's walk back, Trever.

Something was missing in Trever's eyes, too. All that sorrow. He didn't remember Garen, or Ry-Gaul, or Solace. He didn't remember seeing the asteroid blown up in front of his eyes. That was something, at least. Trever had been spared that memory.

Trever's gaze passed over him as though he were a stranger.

Malory introduced him to Clive and Astri. Lune ran down the ramp of the ship and hurried toward Trever, shouting his name. Trever looked startled.

"Guess you're my new family," Trever said. "You don't look so bad."

"And this is Ferus Olin," Malory said. "He's from your homeworld."

Trever turned to him. "Good to meet you."

Ferus couldn't speak.

"Are we going to get this show on the road?" Trever asked. "I can't remember chunks of my old life, so I'm kinda anxious to start on the new one."

Ferus cleared his throat. "Good-bye."

"See you! Hey, whoa, is that our cruiser? Sweet!" Trever hurried toward Astri and Clive's ship. "C'mon, kid!" he called to Lune.

Lune hesitated before turning away. "May the Force be with you," he said to Ferus.

"May the Force be with you, Lune. You would have made a fine Jedi. Take care of Trever. Just don't let him know it."

Lune grinned and ran off.

"I'm not saying good-bye," Clive said. "I have a feeling I'll see you again. You have an annoying habit of popping up when I least expect it."

"You never know," Ferus said.

He embraced Astri, then Clive. Malory climbed into her cruiser. After administering the memory agent to Trever, she had destroyed it. It was too dangerous to keep active while the Empire controlled the galaxy.

He watched Malory's ship rise and join the space traffic. Astri's ship followed.

In his heart, he wished them long lives and as much peace as they could find.

He would never see them again.

CHAPTER TWENTY-ONE

The grasslands of Alderaan were vast and beautiful. Ferus lived on the edge of the great wilderness that lay across the sea from Aldera. Close enough to the city, but not part of it.

Bail had found him a house nestled in a small valley. He had no close neighbors. His cover story was that he was a botanist, working on a great work on the grasses of Alderaan.

His real work was protecting Princess Leia.

He was here not as a bodyguard, but as a safeguard. Just as Obi-Wan watched over Luke from a distance, he would be here if Leia needed him. She would never know him, but he would always be there.

He would make sure that no danger came to her. The daughter of Anakin Skywalker and Padmé Amidala would always be safe.

Ferus stood outside the door of his small dwelling. The sun was on his face and the wind was in his hair, but he didn't feel them. Instead he felt only the memories of all the lives that had touched his, and the people that he'd loved. Trever lived in him, and Roan. The Jedi he had fought beside. The heroes he had known.

Obi-Wan had told him to trust that a rebellion would rise. It would take years, but it would come. Dex's words had comforted him. In his mind, Ferus saw Garen, Solace, and Ry-Gaul, but he also saw new heroes behind them, stepping up to take their places.

Obi-Wan was right about forgiveness. Ferus could feel himself gain a little more each day. He had even forgiven Anakin, for hadn't he come close to the line that Anakin had crossed? Underneath his tunic was a red scar — a brand to remind him that he had touched the dark side of the Force.

Maybe that scar would remind him about the need for compassion. And one day he would able to direct it toward himself.

Obi-Wan had shared some of Qui-Gon Jinn's words with him before he'd left Tatooine.

A Force connection is a gift we honor not only in our hearts, but in our choices.

"You made the choice to live," Obi-Wan had told him. "Now live with honor."

His gaze moved toward the city of Aldera. This was his new home. Ferus knew in his bones that he wouldn't leave this planet alive. These grasslands would hold his spirit one day.

Here he would live, until the day he joined the Force and joined his friends, and Roan, at last. Until then he would trade the life he'd had for this one. He would say good-bye to all the things he'd known.

The journey begins, he told himself. *So go.*